The Violin Players

University of Nebraska Press

Lincoln

The Violin Players

Eileen Bluestone Sherman

The Jewish Publication Society
Philadelphia

© 1998 by Eileen Bluestone Sherman

All rights reserved.

Published by the University of Nebraska
Press as a Jewish Publication Society book.

First Nebraska printing: 2020

Library of Congress
Control Number: 2020943133

Typeset by Varda Graphics, Inc.

For sisters and friends
GAIL, FLOSSIE, LINDA, MICHELE,
CAROL, RUTH, CAROLYN, BETSY, JILL,
AND DIANNE

Contents

The Violin Players

1

The Flight

A LONG LINE OF PASSENGERS crowded the aisle of the airplane. Heaving a sigh of disgust, Melissa Jensen took her place by the window. The teenager's sulking did not go unnoticed as she tried to find a comfortable position for her long legs crunched in between the narrow rows of seats.

"Ah, come on, Melly," coaxed her dad. "It's not going to be all that bad." He grabbed her black violin case and placed it next to his briefcase in the compartment above their seats.

"You actually might enjoy yourself," added Melissa's mother as she carefully positioned the airline pillow behind her short red hair.

"Give me a break," Melissa mumbled under her breath.

Anita Jensen heard the remark but she ignored it. To finish all her packing, Melissa's mom had started at 4 A.M. She, for one, was grateful to be on board. With her eyelids drooping over her big green eyes, she mumbled, "Wake me when we land."

As Melissa buckled her seat belt, she was still trying to understand her father's decision to leave New York and go teach in the Midwest. Of course, she knew all the facts. Six weeks ago, her dad's literary agent had received a call from one very anxious theater professor in Missouri. The school's playwriting instructor needed to take a sudden leave of absence, and a mutual friend had suggested Melissa's dad as a substitute teacher. The professor nervously inquired whether Michael Jensen might be available to teach the last seven weeks of the school's fall semester. As an incentive, the theater department promised to produce Michael Jensen's new comedy in the spring. Melissa knew her father normally would never have considered the offer, but just one day earlier, the group of producers who had promised to finance her father's new comedy in Boston and then tour the show around the country in preparation for a New York opening had decided to scrap the project entirely. Suddenly, the Midwest didn't sound so remote for a premiere. Still, Melissa had been amazed when her father had grabbed the deal. "But, Dad! Henryville? It's the middle of nowhere," Melissa had protested when she realized her dad was quite serious.

"Look, Melly," he had finally conceded, "I'd rather some New York producer jump on the bandwagon. But listen, this could do the trick. Henryville's not so isolated. It's a little more than an hour outside Kansas City. Besides, I just keep thinking of what happened to Bill Landen. Four years ago, he tried out his play at a little-known college theater in Arizona. Now he's got a smash hit on Broadway!"

Ever since Melissa could remember her father had been trying to get a play on Broadway. It wasn't as if Michael Jensen was unknown to other directors and actors. His comedies were very popular at many of the finest regional and dinner theaters throughout the country and they had even been shown on cable television. Unfortunately, devoted audiences in Fort Wayne, Indiana, or even TV executives did not carry much influence with Broadway producers. Melissa decided her father must be awfully desperate to consider sacrificing seven months of their lives.

"It's not a sacrifice," he kept insisting. "It's an adventure that somehow will pay off. You'll see."

All Melissa could see was a gray November day outside her window. The pilot's voice came over the loudspeaker. "Flight attendants, please prepare for takeoff." Melissa took a final glimpse of the New York skyline while her large green eyes, shaped just like her mother's, struggled to fight back the tears.

It wasn't like she had never left New York before this. "Melly," her mom was fond of saying, "has been flying since infancy. Our careers demand it."

A noted artist, Melissa's mother received dozens of invitations each year to exhibit and speak about her portrait painting. Likewise, her father was often asked to address aspiring writers or to be present for an opening night. Whenever possible Melissa gladly skipped a day or two of school to accompany her parents. Luckily, she had always excelled in the classroom, and her teachers were usually very understanding about make-up work. Naturally, summer was the best time for any extended travel. Just last August, her mother's commission to paint the governor's family had been a perfect excuse to plan a family holiday in Maine. One July they had even traveled to England. For Melissa, boarding an airplane felt as natural as French braiding her thick blond hair every morning. Yes, normally, she loved flying. But this trip was different.

This trip meant leaving her two best girlfriends for the remainder of their junior year. This trip meant forfeiting her place as concertmaster of the school orchestra. This trip meant giving up the title of captain of the debating team. Worst of all, this trip meant no school musical, after the director had announced that Melissa Jensen would be playing the leading role.

Melissa knew her father was not oblivious to her disappointment. "I talked to your grandparents," he had told her one week before their departure. "If you want to stay in New York, they'd be thrilled to have you."

Melissa had declined the offer. "I would miss you a lot," is what she told him. But that was only partially true. There was one other reason for her decision. Melissa did not want to live with Ida and Joseph Janiwitz.

As much as she loved her grandmother and grandfather, she often wondered how her father had survived childhood in an Orthodox Jewish household. It seemed so full of rules and regulations. Ida Janiwitz kept a strictly kosher kitchen. Joseph Janiwitz prayed daily at the synagogue. No matter the weather, every Saturday morning they walked to and from the synagogue. As a little girl, Melissa remembered that twelve-minute walk in the bitter cold or pouring rain as absolute torture. Saturday afternoons were equally painful. No movies. No card games. No television. No telephone. No writing. No shopping. No radio. On Shabbat, not even the flipping of a light switch was permitted in Ida and Joseph's apartment. No, Melissa was not prepared to become an observant Jew just so she could star in a high school production of *Grease*. Besides, what good would it do her? Living at her grandparents' house, she wouldn't be able to attend the Saturday rehearsals or, for that matter, perform in the Saturday matinee.

Melissa had always thought it quite natural that once at Berkeley her father had abandoned his parents' old-fashioned ways. She knew he had never meant to hurt them, but she also credited him with enough sense to want to fit in with the rest of America. True, many directors, actors, and other playwrights were Jewish, but none that her parents knew seemed the least bit observant. "Most," her father once commented, "do not even belong to a synagogue." Of course, that did not impress her grandmother who never gave up the notion that one day her granddaughter would attend Hebrew school. Melissa listened to many conversations at her grandparents' dinner table and often noticed that her father tried to make a joke of their concern. "Don't worry, Ma," he had once good-naturedly teased his perplexed mother. "Melly knows who she is. Right, kiddo?" and he had looked over and winked at his daughter. "How can she forget? We live in New York, the Kingdom of Kosher Delis!"

Melissa had laughed right along as her father flashed that endearing smile she had inherited from him. But her grandmother had not been amused by either her son's glib remarks or his decision years ago to change his name from Janiwitz to Jensen. "Kibbitz all you like," she had answered him while looking directly at her amused granddaughter. "Matzah balls and bagels do not make a Jew. Ignorance, Melissa, is a terrible, terrible curse. And another thing," she had scolded her son, "Christmas tree in a Jewish home? I never heard of such a thing! It's a shanda."

Later, when Melissa had asked her father what "shanda" meant, they had sat down together and had a long discus-

sion. "The Yiddish word means 'disgrace,' and your grandmother thinks I should be ashamed of myself. But honey, I'm
not. Your mother grew up without learning a single word of
Hebrew or attending a synagogue. Being different from the
non-Jewish kids was never one of your mother's childhood
worries. In fact, your grandparents in San Francisco were so
modern they simply called their tree a 'Hanukkah bush.'
Trust me. It never hurt your mother. In fact, I don't think
there is any woman more intelligent, beautiful, talented, and
remarkable in the whole world. I pray you grow up to be like
her in every way. Still," he had confessed to Melissa, "I don't
want to make Grandma and Grandpa Janiwitz angry. It
makes me sad that they can't understand. I do love them."

As Melissa sat and remembered these comments, she
fumed even more. Why did her father always seem so sensi-
tive to everyone's feelings but hers? When he suddenly
reached out to take her hand, she pulled away from him.

"Hey, kiddo, take pity on your old man. In all our years
together, have I ever let you down? I make a prediction that
six months from now you'll be wishing we could stay longer."

Without the slightest hint of expression, Melissa answered,
"The playwright has a vivid imagination."

"It speaks!" teased her father. Then, as if on cue, her
mother made a funny, gurgling sound in her sleep. No matter
how hard she tried, Melissa could not suppress a giggle.

Her father seized the moment. "Hey, how about a fish
tournament?" He pulled a box of cards out of his jacket
pocket.

"You must be kidding," scoffed Melissa as she grabbed the
deck from her father. "But I'll take you up on a game of
poker." She started to shuffle the cards. "So? What are you
waiting for? Get out your change."

The first time they had played this game, Melissa had been only ten. One of her father's plays had been produced in a small theater outside London, and after its opening the family had spent the rest of the summer touring the English countryside. On the long plane ride home, Melissa had been fidgety, so her father had entertained her by teaching her poker. She had learned quickly and in the next five years managed to outbluff every one of her dad's Thursday night poker buddies. Melissa was not only a skilled card player. She was a natural actress. Only once did this potent combination get her into serious trouble.

Melissa was in sixth grade when her mother received a phone call from Mrs. O'Connor, the school principal, who reported that Melissa had been suspended. When the Jensens had rushed down to their daughter's school, they were informed that their child, a "4.0" honor roll student, a class representative, and the editor of the student newsletter, had been setting up poker games during study hall. To make matters worse, when one student had demanded her money back because she needed her bus fare home, Melissa had refused to return any winnings. Only after her one-day suspension and an apology to the traumatized classmate had Melissa been allowed to return to school.

As Melissa dealt the next hand, her father reminded her of the incident. "Puh-leeze! It's been a long time since sixth grade. But I still insist I was the one victimized," Melissa responded indignantly.

"I just don't want any calls from your new school," her father said.

"Not a chance. There's nothing very scandalous about a game of solitaire," Melissa said with exasperation.

"Why? You don't expect to make friends?"

"Like I'm really going to have something in common with these geeks! They probably all milk cows and feed chickens."

Michael Jensen shrugged. "I guess there will be some farm kids. That might be interesting. But trust me. It's not how you imagine. The town is charming. The people I met were very educated. Cultured. Hey! They must have some taste. They want to produce my play!" The playwright winked and then followed it up with one of his signature grins.

Melissa responded by sticking out her tongue. His attempt to lift her spirits was irritating. She didn't need to meet new people. She simply needed Jill and Anna, her two best friends. Jill played cello, Anna played flute, and Melissa played violin. All three were only freshmen when they were selected for the school orchestra. In the past two years, the three had become inseparable. Each friend had begged Melissa to stay with her in New York.

Of course, Melissa knew Jill's offer was out of the question. Her parents were newly divorced. With Jill and her brother living with their mother in New York during the week and then commuting to their father's Westport, Connecticut, home on weekends, their lives had become rather complicated. They certainly didn't need Melissa tagging along every day.

Anna's household was more like Melissa's, but Anna was the oldest of four daughters. Mr. and Mrs. Wu, two highly accomplished musicians, were also actively involved in the high school. Mrs. Wu served as chairwoman of the school's cultural arts committee, and Mr. Wu often appeared as a guest conductor for the school orchestra.

Just a couple of days before leaving, Melissa had mentioned the possibility of staying at Anna's but the Jensens had vigorously opposed the idea. The stay would have been too long. They argued that the Wus had demanding careers and a hectic family life, so they certainly didn't need another child for half a year. Melissa's parents agreed that she should either stay with her grandparents or join them in Missouri. Neither of these choices suited Melissa. So, as she watched her father study his cards, she could not forgive him for making her so unhappy.

"I'll see you and raise you a nickel," her dad declared.

Melissa tossed her cards onto the tray table. "I don't want to play anymore." She frowned and turned toward the window. Mr. Jensen tried to reason with his daughter.

"Melissa, you're not even giving it a chance. You know new places can open up a whole world of opportunity. I mean, look at me. I never would have met your mother if I hadn't left the East."

"How can you compare the two? You went to California," snapped Melissa.

"So how do you know something or someone isn't waiting for you in the Midwest?"

"You're soooo embarrassing," Melissa said. "Do you actual-ly believe I could even be mildly interested in anyone who grew up on *Little House on the Prairie*?" Michael Jensen ignor-ed the teenage sarcasm. He picked up the cards and placed them back in the box. "I think I'll nap, too." He pushed his seat backward and closed his eyes.

"Oh, great!" thought Melissa. "They drag me on to this airplane and then desert me." The last time she felt this terrible, she had just broken up with Paul.

The thought of Paul made her feel even worse. How she wished things had turned out differently. The two had gone out for a year. She had liked him more than any boy she had ever known. This past summer, she had written to him every day from Maine. But when she returned Melissa found out that Paul Whitney had a new girlfriend. Only her grandmother had celebrated.

"Thank heaven," Melissa had overheard her grandmother tell her mother. "I try not to interfere, but I was beside myself. Do you realize that for a whole year she dated a Gentile?"

"Mom, you overreact," Anita had calmly answered her mother-in-law. "Melly's only fifteen."

"Five or fifteen, the boy must be Jewish."

Melissa had been hearing this same lecture from her grandmother since first grade, when she had announced she was in love with a boy on her swimming team. Of course, Melissa knew lots of Jewish boys. They just weren't all that interesting.

Still, out of respect, Melissa never argued with her grandmother. Besides, she knew she could never change her grandmother's opinion. But, of course, neither would her own opinion change. After all, it did not matter to her that Paul wasn't Jewish. It only mattered that he had hurt her. For a moment, she allowed herself to consider her father's comment. Maybe she was destined to meet someone this winter.

The pilot's voice boomed over the loudspeaker. "Well, folks, we should be arriving at the Kansas City International Airport shortly. I'm afraid, however, we're flying into a storm. I expect we'll hit some turbulence, so keep those seat belts fastened. We're scheduled to land in about forty-five minutes."

Melissa's daydreaming stopped. This was really happening. The plane would be down on the ground, and she would be thrust into an unknown world. She realized her parents did not appreciate the ordeal ahead of her. After all, both of them had a cozy niche waiting for them. Both had been asked to teach at the college. They would be welcomed into the fold. But what about her? Sure, she had always been an honors student, but coming to a completely new school system this late in the term was a challenge she did not relish. How did her parents expect her to maintain her perfect 4.0 when logically she was already weeks behind her classmates? No teachers knew her. No one knew her. She'd have to prove herself all over again. The thought made her sick to her stomach.

Surprisingly, her mother and father continued to sleep peacefully. They were oblivious to the turmoil in the atmosphere. Even worse, they were oblivious to the turmoil building inside their daughter.

2

Rich Man's Alley

AS SOON AS SHE SPOTTED THE SIGN with their names on it, Melissa raised her hand and started waving to the young man waiting at the gate. Even from a distance, she could see the boy was very good-looking.

"Hi, I'm Chris Brown. Dad couldn't get out of the faculty meeting. It's a weekly thing. Dad's got one every Thursday afternoon. I'm supposed to offer his apology. And since Mom is setting up for tomorrow's PTA luncheon at the high school, I was elected chauffeur." The boy reached out to shake hands with Michael Jensen. "I know my dad's real excited you're here."

As they were walking toward the carousel to claim their baggage, Anita whispered in her daughter's ear, "I wonder how old he is." Melissa shrugged with a pretended indifference, but the boy's broad shoulders and thick wavy blond hair did not go unnoticed—nor did the two dimples on either side of his friendly smile. Everyone carried something, but Chris single-handedly picked up three of their heaviest pieces of luggage and continued to carry on a pleasant conversation while lugging the suitcases to the parking lot. By the time they reached the station wagon, Melissa knew that Christopher Brown was almost eighteen years old, a senior at Henryville High School, and the captain of the football team.

"I'm praying for a football scholarship to either Michigan or Alabama," he told them as he pulled out of the airport onto an almost empty highway toward Henryville. Otherwise, it's the old junior college for me. Faculty kids go free. Lucky Mom and Dad," he chuckled. "Most of my friends plan to stick around, so it wouldn't be so bad. I know my girlfriend would like it."

Looking disinterested in the back seat, Melissa heaved a quiet sigh. She stopped listening to the friendly chatter around her and stared out the window. "Miles and miles of farmland. Nothing else," she thought. She suddenly realized Chris was speaking to her. "My sister, Kathy, wanted to make sure I invite you to a slumber party she's having for her girlfriends after the game Friday night. She's a junior, too. Like you."

"Yeah," Melissa mumbled. After a momentary pause she added, "Thanks, but better not count on me. By tomorrow night I'll be zonked. Jet lag. First day of school, you know what I mean. I'm exhausted already." Her voice trailed off into a whisper.

But Chris was persistent. "Sorry. Can't take 'No' for an answer. Besides, you'll have the weekend to sleep in. Trust me. It's gonna be great," he argued. "Everyone's really anxious to meet you."

"Me?" Melissa's tone revealed a hint of skepticism.

"Sure. You're hot news. Most of us can only dream about life in the 'Big Apple.' Hey, my sister Kathy was green with envy when she couldn't come to the airport but the squad called a practice. She's co-captain of the cheerleaders," he explained. "Wouldn't look too good if she cut."

Melissa would never have admitted it but she was flattered. To think, people were actually waiting to meet her. Suddenly, Melissa was smiling and for the first time that day, her green eyes sparkled. "Tell Kathy, it's really very nice of her to include me," she offered in her sweetest voice.

About ninety minutes later, as they approached the center of town, Melissa was again pleasantly surprised. Refurbished red brick buildings from the turn of the century lined each side of Main Street, and on each corner stood a street light designed to look like the old-fashioned gas lamps of the 1890s. Although the architecture evoked thoughts of an earlier time, the merchandise for sale was very much a reflection of the present. Melissa hastily noted a computer center, a video shop, a CD store and a warehouse for all the latest high-tech sound systems, as well as a store front advertising body building equipment. In the center of all this "modern living" was Sarah's Sweet Shop. When Melissa saw a crowd of teenagers pushing their way inside, she concluded the ice cream parlor must be the hangout.

In New York, she and her friends usually met at the deli across the street from her school. But she already knew there were no delis or bagel shops in Henryville. Even her father admitted he would miss his lox and bagel with cream cheese on Sunday mornings. Melissa, who hated most fish, figured that was the least of her problems.

As they turned the corner from Main Street, Chris pointed

out the City Hall and the town's perfectly manicured park across the road. Then he said, "You're two weeks too late."

"Too late for what?" asked Melissa's mother as she searched for her lipstick and compact inside her overpacked pocketbook.

"The leaves. They've mostly fallen by now. When they turn, it's unbelievable."

"Wait till you see the college, Anita. I tell you it's like a set from one of those old movies," Melissa's father added.

"As a matter of fact," interrupted Chris, "a big deal Hollywood director was supposed to shoot a film on the campus. But the project's been scrapped. They say the money dried up."

"That's show biz," her father sighed. In his own career, Melissa's father had suffered several major disappointments because producers had miscalculated expenses. Luckily, there was little time to recall any of those unfortunate moments.

Chris pulled over to the curb and announced, "Home, sweet home!"

"Wow!" exclaimed Melissa as she stared up at the three-story stone mansion.

"Great place. Dates back to 1910. The college bought it in the mid eighties. They've really spruced it up. We use it for all sorts of functions. All the old homes on this block are owned by the school now. Very convenient. You're only two short blocks from the main campus."

"Perfect " said Anita Jensen.

"Wait till you see the inside. The college really knocked themselves out when they redid it. Fantastic place for a party. Last three Decembers my mom's hosted the Christmas tea for faculty here. Since you'll be living here, I know she wouldn't want to impose on your privacy. I suppose she'll have to scout around for a new location."

"Nonsense," Melissa's father replied. "We always have a party in New York. Isn't that right, darling?" He gave his wife a definite look, and she quickly picked up her cue.

"Tomorrow I'll call your mother, Chris, and mention it. Before you know it, the holidays will be here and I'd love to help however I can."

"You three can sit here and chat about eggnog and petit fours," Melissa said impatiently, "but I'm ready to check out the place." She jumped out of the car and ran up the flight of porch steps. Chris ran after her.

"Can't get in without these," he taunted and dangled the set of house keys high in the air. Melissa leaped up to grab them. She was quick enough to catch his fist, but not strong enough to release the keys from his grip. She kept trying.

"Um. We heard you East coast girls are aggressive," he teased. His deep blue eyes looked straight into hers.

Slowly, the corners of Melissa's mouth turned upward into a coy smile. No way would she retreat. "Hope your girlfriend isn't the jealous type." She meant the remark as a joke but Chris did not smile.

Michael Jensen interrupted. "I thought we were going inside." Melissa stepped aside to let Chris open the door. He gestured for Mr. and Mrs. Jensen to enter first. Then he turned to Melissa and said, "Welcome home."

Melissa, who had grown up in a Manhattan West Side co-op with two small bedrooms, let out tiny gasps of disbelief. Each room, even the front hall, was grand and elegant, with high ceilings, carved moldings, and glossy wood floors. She counted the chairs. The dining room table seated twenty-four people. And there were two staircases. She ran up and down both of them. The front staircase was winding with a heavy brass railing. The rear one allowed a direct route from the kitchen to the six upstairs bedrooms. After inspecting each one, Melissa returned downstairs and requested the ivory bedroom with the canopy bed.

"Whichever one you want," Anita said gleefully. She was as overwhelmed as her daughter. Not even Michael Jensen had expected such majestic accommodations.

Then Chris escorted them to one end of the living room. The family sighed in unison when Chris threw open the hand-painted French glass doors leading to a large open room with two opulent chandeliers. "In 1911," Chris informed them, "this street was dubbed 'Rich Man's Alley.' You were considered a poor relation if you didn't have your own personal ballroom."

Anita, who was already imagining how she would decorate for the December festivities, told her husband, "I can see why this place is perfect for a college reception."

Chris agreed. "Yup. Parties and roller skating," he chuckled as he winked at Melissa.

"Really?" she asked.

"Please don't give her any ideas. We're only tenants here, young lady," Michael Jensen reminded his daughter.

"You don't have to worry, Mr. Jensen. The college is so thrilled to have you, they wouldn't care if you skated on the ceiling. I mean the Board has been knocking themselves out to try to impress you. Wait till you see what's in the garage."

Chris slipped his hand into his pocket and pulled out a set of keys. He was addressing her father but Melissa listened carefully. "The two brass ones open the front deadbolt and back door," Chris explained.

"What about the silver key?" Michael Jensen wanted to know.

"It's your wheels."

"A car!" Melissa shrieked. She had almost forgotten! In New York, Melissa had decided the only good part of this bargain was access to an automobile. Maybe, finally, someone would teach her how to drive a car.

"It's out back in the four-car garage. Unfortunately, the college only provides one 'free vehicle per visiting professor,' he added sarcastically.

"One more than we had in Manhattan," her mother said with glee. Melissa could tell from her mother's impish grin how pleased she was to have a car again. As a former Californian, her mother had driven everywhere before relocating to New York. Although she knew her parents could afford to buy a car and had discussed the matter often, to Melissa's disappointment, they had always decided against it. "Cars are just too much of a hassle in the city," her father and mother agreed.

"By the way, I'll need directions to get to the high school tomorrow. I don't want Melly to be late her first day."

"I have that covered, Mrs. Jensen." Then Chris turned to Melissa. "Kathy and I plan to be here at seven o'clock sharp tomorrow morning. That way, you'll have time to meet some of the gang."

"Great," Melissa said.

Neither parent missed the smile on Chris's face as he bid farewell to their daughter. After the boy departed, Michael Jensen could not resist teasing Melissa. "To think that you almost had me feeling sorry for you! We're in Henryville less than an hour and you have the captain of the football team at your beck and call."

"Puh-leeze," Melissa answered with exaggerated indignation. "You heard him. He has a girlfriend."

"But not one from the 'Big Apple,'" mocked her father with a good-natured chuckle.

"Stop your teasing, Michael," scolded Melissa's mother. "Now, folks, we probably need to make a shopping list."

Melissa groaned as she inspected the cupboards and saw only some paper goods, a couple of sponges, and dish detergent.

"OK. Time to take a spin around the town and find a grocery store," her father agreed.

Melissa frowned. "Do I have to go? I'm exhausted. Remember you both slept on the airplane." She wasn't quite as tired as she pretended. She just didn't want to accompany her parents. Even though their new house was a bona fide mansion and Chris Brown was a bona fide high school football captain, she refused to forgive them so easily. After all, they still had dragged her away from all those teachers who adored her in New York. Anticipating the hours of grueling make-up work to catch up in her new classes was enough reason for her to want to stay in bed permanently. To accentuate her fatigue, she started to yawn, making a loud, high-pitched sigh.

"Enough," said her mother. "We get the picture, but aren't you even curious about the car?" Melissa certainly was curious. Throughout all those weeks of sobbing and screaming protests, Melissa could see only one positive reason for leaving New York. She bolted out the back door.

The shiny black Saab with its burgundy leather interior was almost as impressive as the house. Melissa jumped into the driver's seat. "Honey, I think Melly is trying to tell us something," laughed her father.

Mrs. Jensen had already thought about driving lessons for her daughter. When she mentioned the idea, Melissa's face beamed.

"Honest?" shrieked Melissa. "Well, how 'bout we begin right now?"

"Not until this March when you turn sixteen, my dear. Besides, I thought you were tired," said her mother.

"To go food shopping. But I'm wide awake for a driving lesson. Come on. I looked it up. You only have to be fifteen to get a permit out here." Melissa looked up at her mother with her big, hopeful eyes.

"I don't think so. Come on, Michael, before it gets dark. I don't want to get lost. Coming, Melissa?"

"No, thanks," she pouted. "I'll unpack or curl up on one of the beds. We have enough," she said.

"OK. But stay put till we get back," her father ordered.

Melissa watched her parents turn the corner and then returned to the back door. She turned the knob and expected the door to fling open. It didn't. After three attempts, she tried the front door. That did not budge either. The doors were locked.

Luckily, Melissa was still wearing her jacket. The cool autumn air was getting chillier as she sat on the steps and silently reviewed the situation. Unfortunately, the only house keys were dangling from the car ignition, which at the moment was cruising the streets of Henryville. Well, she wasn't going to sit there and become an icicle. Melissa decided to take a walk.

She double checked her new home address, "189 Willow Lane," and whispered it to herself as she began down the street past all the grand houses. Almost every one had a sign in front of it. Department of Journalism. Department of Humanities. Department of Education. Each house had its own distinct character, but was equally majestic.

Melissa turned the corner and faced the main campus. As

much as she hated to admit it, her father had not exaggerated. With its old ivy-covered buildings and massive oak trees, the college looked wonderful.

Melissa took herself on a private tour. She explored the admissions building and school cafeteria. She peeked inside the dance studio, browsed through the library, and, for a few moments, hid in back of the dark theater during a rehearsal of *A Streetcar Named Desire*. The students were quite convincing in their roles. Melissa would have enjoyed watching more, but at the close of the scene the director called for a fifteen-minute break for costume fittings. Disappointed, Melissa left by a side exit.

Outside again, Melissa eyed the bleachers and decided to walk over to the baseball diamond. The sight made her smile. Although she hadn't played much ball this past summer up in Maine, Melissa remained proud of the fact that, for three consecutive seasons at her beloved summer camp, she had been her camp's star outfielder.

"How odd! They're having practice in November," she thought as she watched two figures at home plate. From a distance, she saw a tall young man pick up the bat and swing at the air. An older black gentleman, still looking very fit, was adjusting the younger man's shoulders, elbows, and hips. Then the gray-haired coach ran back to the pitcher's mound and threw the ball.

The pitch was fast. The boy swung and smacked the ball solidly into left outfield. Both batter and pitcher watched it fly toward Melissa. When Melissa realized the ball was coming right at her, she forgot she was a stranger on a strange college campus and instinctively leaped up in the air. The ball landed snugly inside her two cupped hands. Its impact stung her bare flesh, but she was so proud of her catch that she ignored the pain and confidently threw the ball back to the pitcher's mound. The man caught it and motioned for Melissa to approach him. The curious batter also ran up to the mound.

"Nice catch, young lady, and very impressive outfielding. That's quite an arm you've got there," said the man. "Where did you learn to throw like that?"

Melissa beamed with pride. "Softball was my sport at camp."

"Shouldn't give it up," the strikingly handsome boy said. His dark, powerful eyes mesmerized Melissa. She tried to regain her composure but she remained flustered.

"Thanks," is all she could think to say to him. After another awkward pause, she said, "Gotta go." As she ran back into the outfield, she remembered to turn around and shout, "That was a great hit."

She didn't stop running until she knew she was out of sight. Melissa saw the library steps. Out of breath, she sat down and let her head fall to her knees. "Well, I certainly made a complete fool out of myself," she thought while shaking her bowed head. She felt so embarrassed. "He must have thought I was a total ditz. Couldn't think of anything to say. And staring at him like that. Oh, stop being so hard on yourself," was her next thought. "After all, you did catch the ball."

She checked her watch and figured she had at least another twenty-five minutes before her parents would return. She went into the library to read. A half-hour later, Melissa started for home. When she reached the corner of Willow Lane, she heard a car honking and looked to her left. A voice from behind the wheel called out to her, "Didn't mean to startle you. Just wanted to tell you again what a great catch that was!"

The late afternoon sun was shining directly in her face. Melissa put her hand up to her forehead and squinted. Because of the blinding sun in her eyes, she could not see the driver very clearly but knew it was the ballplayer. All she could really see was his dark, wavy hair, which looked a little wild. She liked it. She also liked his old red Mustang.

"Just lucky," she said modestly.

"I don't think so. You looked pretty good out there. You heard what Gus said and he never hands out compliments unless they're deserved. Great man. Coaches for the college. He was giving me a few pointers. You know, he used to play professional baseball."

"Really? Which team?" Melissa was genuinely impressed.

"Well, it was before the teams were integrated. Ever heard of the Kansas City Monarchs?"

Melissa shook her head. "But don't go by me."

Before the boy could explain further, a car pulled up behind him and the driver started pounding on the horn.

"Well, I guess we'll have to continue this another time," he said. "See you around."

As the car drove away, Melissa realized she didn't even know the boy's name, but she was flattered that he had stopped to talk to her. Maybe, she hadn't seemed too goofy after all.

When Melissa's parents returned, they were surprised to find their daughter on the porch. "You locked me out," she announced to them. Melissa knew she could pretend to be irritated or simply tell the truth. "It worked out fine. I gave myself a little tour of the campus."

"What do you think?" Melissa's dad anxiously asked her.

Melissa hated to give him the satisfaction but she answered honestly.

"I admit it," she said. "The place is gorgeous. Still, I don't want to live here permanently."

"Hey, I told you one of the plusses of attending high school in the Midwest is the closing date. By the end of May, classes are over and we're on the first jet home," her father assured her. He raised his right hand as if to take a pledge. "You have my solemn oath. Now, how about unpacking those suitcases?"

Melissa dutifully marched upstairs and started the awesome task of organizing her new room. Before she knew it, her suitcases were empty but almost everything remained on the bed, on top of the desk, or sitting in piles on the floor. When her mother called her down for dinner, Melissa merely closed the door behind her. She hoped the task would seem less of an ordeal after a good meal. That evening, after dinner, she sat alone at the kitchen table and wrote to both Jill and Anna. In her letters she described her new house, the car, and the two boys. "Maybe it won't be as terrible as I expected," she confessed. "Still, please try to come out over winter break. Otherwise, I'll never survive," she wrote them.

She was just sealing Jill's letter when the telephone rang. She ran to answer it.

"Hi!" boomed the voice at the other end. "It's Chris."

"Hello," Melissa said happily.

"So, are you ready for tomorrow?" Chris asked.

"Not really," Melissa replied. "I'm still organizing my things. I didn't realize how much I brought with me."

"Better hop to it," ordered Chris. "We're gonna be at your place real early. You're gonna need some extra time to pick up your schedule, get your locker assignment, and stuff like that. Classes begin at 7:40. Kathy hopes you two get the same lunch."

"That would be nice," Melissa agreed.

"Yeah, I guess. Actually, I think it would be nicer if you had my lunch period." If Chris had been in the room, he would have seen the sparkle in her eyes. "All right. I'll let you get back to work. See you tomorrow," and Chris said goodbye.

No sooner did Melissa hang up the receiver than the phone rang again. She figured Chris had forgotten to tell her something. "Yeah?" she answered.

"Melissa, is that you? What kind of way is that to answer the telephone?"

"Grandma! Hi! I'm sorry. I thought it was someone else."

"No, darling, it's your grandmother. How was the flight?"

"Fine, I guess," Melissa said. "Wait till you see this house. I swear it's a mansion."

"I heard. Your father called earlier and told me all about it. But do me a favor. Don't swear. It doesn't sound nice."

"Yes, Grandma," Melissa answered dutifully.

"I just wanted to call you and wish you well for your first day of school tomorrow," Melissa's grandmother continued. "Remember, if you don't like it, you can fly right back to Manhattan. Grandpa and I would love to have you."

"Thanks, but oddly enough, I'm actually looking forward to tomorrow." Melissa wanted to hang up so she could finish unpacking.

"You know, darling. I have a neighbor," said Mrs. Janiwitz. "Shirley Rosenstein. Lives upstairs in my building. Anyway, she has family in Kansas City. I think that's about sixty miles from where you are. She says the town is lovely and with a very nice Jewish community. You could make some friends. Ask your mother to look into it."

At that moment, Anita entered the kitchen. "Here's Mom now," is all Melissa said as she quickly handed the receiver to her mother and headed straight up the back stairway. Melissa ran into her room and closed the door.

Her shoulders drooped. Where to begin? The room looked like the debris from a deadly tornado. Clothes, books, shoes, jewelry, hair supplies—all kinds of personal items were everywhere. Before Chris's phone call, Melissa had been content to procrastinate cleaning up until the weekend. Now she was motivated. To look her best tomorrow, she would have to organize tonight.

When Melissa finally undressed for bed, turned off the overhead light, and collapsed onto the crisp, clean sheets of the canopy bed, she felt a nervous tingling inside. What a surprise! The day she had dreaded for weeks had turned out to be quite extraordinary. How could she ever have guessed about this fantastic house, the car, or Chris Brown? And what about the baseball player?

"Yes, what about him?" Melissa whispered to herself in the dark. "No, Grandma, I'm going to stick around for a while. Dad was right. This is an adventure." She remembered her grandmother's comment about Kansas City and chuckled. "Poor Grandma won't ever give up on her crusade to find me a Jewish boyfriend. I hate to break it to her, but right now being Jewish is the last thing on my mind."

3

Henryville High

AS PROMISED, CHRIS ARRIVED at her house that Friday morning at seven o'clock sharp. Melissa squeezed into the back seat of the Browns' station wagon, and Chris started the introductions, "This is Melissa Jensen, everyone."

Melissa nodded with a friendly smile at the girl and boy beside her. Another girl was sitting in front, next to Chris, but Melissa couldn't see her face.

"Hi. I'm Kathy Brown," said the bubbly teen seated right next to Melissa. There was no mistaking Kathy for anyone other than Chris's sister. She had the same thick, blond hair, the same piercing blue eyes, and the same two adorable dimples on either side of a naturally radiant smile. Like her brother, she was seldom at a loss for words. "I think it's so exciting you're from New York," Kathy gushed. "I can't wait to move there."

"In her dreams," mumbled the boy beside Kathy.

"Quiet, Johnny," she scolded as she nudged him gently with her elbow. "Nobody believes me, but I plan to go to Manhattan right after high school. Everyone thinks I'm crazy, but I'm determined to be a Rockette. I bet you get to Radio City Music Hall a lot."

Melissa smiled. "Not much lately, but I used to love it when I was younger."

"A girl from my dancing school auditioned and was offered a job," Kathy proudly informed the group.

"You're kidding. Who?" asked the red headed girl sitting in the passenger seat next to Chris. She turned around slightly to look at Kathy, but avoided any eye contact with Melissa. Then she turned to the front again. From the way she clung to Chris's arm at the steering wheel, Melissa surmised that the redhead was his girlfriend.

"Helen Winters," answered Kathy.

"Wow!" said Johnny. "My brother dated her." As he jutted out his massive chest with masculine pride, his lips parted slightly, and Melissa noticed a slight gap between his front teeth. She also noticed his unusually large hands. He caught Melissa looking at him. "Hi, there. I'm Johnny McGraw."

"Johnny, along with Chris, is one of the stars of the football team," Kathy announced.

"Yep, he's a definite threat out there on the field. Aren't you, Johnny?" Chris added with genuine respect.

"True. Football is my claim to fame, but my real passion is wrestling." Suddenly Johnny was staring directly at Melissa. "Do you like wrestlers, Jensen?" Johnny asked.

Melissa shrugged indifferently. "Depends on the wrestler, McGraw."

Chris bit down on his lip to keep from laughing. "I warned you, Johnny. New York girls are quick."

The redhead let go of Chris's arm and turned to glare back at Melissa. Although she was smiling, her expression revealed a quiet hostility. "It must be cool to have famous parents," the girl in the front seat said. "I suppose you don't get bored tagging along."

Melissa mimicked the girl's condescending air. "I'm sorry. I don't think I caught your name."

"That's Tina," Kathy blurted out while the redhead turned to the front again and inched closer to Chris. Kathy looked at Melissa and rolled her eyes.

Later, when the two girls were alone in the hallway, Kathy cornered Melissa. "Don't pay any attention to Tina," Kathy advised. "She's so obnoxious and she's consumed with jealousy. Since yesterday, Chris has done nothing but talk about you and your father and mother. Granted, Tina's a knockout and worships Chris like a god, but I wish he'd dump her. She gets on my nerves."

Both girls chuckled. Then Melissa inquired, "What's the story with Johnny?"

Kathy blushed. "I'm working on him. I know he's just as obnoxious as Tina but what can I say? Love is blind. I've had a secret crush on him since he moved here in junior high school. He and Chris are real good buddies."

"That should come in handy," teased Melissa.

"Yes and no. I'm afraid he just thinks of me as Chris's kid sister. How 'bout you? Got someone in New York?"

"Nope," is all Melissa said, but Kathy detected the loneliness in her voice.

"I figure it's pretty scary to come to a new place, especially after the school year has begun. But don't worry. Everyone is really curious about you. You'll do just fine." Kathy's reassurance bolstered Melissa's confidence.

The five-minute warning bell rang. The girls hurried into the school office. Mrs. Peters ordered Kathy to return to homeroom, but before leaving, Kathy hastily eyed Melissa's schedule. "We only have English together," moaned Kathy. She looked up and met the vice-principal's cold stare. "I'll see you second period," whispered Kathy and made a quick exit.

Once alone with the vice-principal, Melissa noticed that Mrs. Peters's manner softened. Her professional concern put Melissa at ease, and Melissa's first impulse was to like this principal whose tone was authoritative but reassuring. Melissa decided the attractive woman chose to wear her brunette hair in a French twist to give herself a more mature look. Even so, Melissa figured the principal couldn't be any older than her early thirties.

"I'm happy to have you at our high school, Melissa. I understand this sudden change must be terribly difficult. Please feel free to come to me with any problems. Of course, I don't foresee any. Your records indicate that you're an honors student and are quite accomplished in the arts. I think you'll find our school has a lot to offer you."

Melissa was doubtful, but she appreciated Mrs. Peters's sincerity. She listened politely.

"We were told you play the violin and also enjoy acting. I've taken the liberty of placing you in our school orchestra, as well as the drama elective."

"Won't I have to audition?"

Mrs. Peters smiled. "Our student population is less than three hundred, dear, and most prefer athletics. Believe me. You'll be welcomed with open arms."

Melissa's expression easily betrayed her private thoughts.

"Don't misunderstand," Mrs. Peters assured her, "some of our students are very talented."

Melissa had already decided otherwise. Any pitiful orchestra that snatched up anyone who claimed to play an instrument couldn't possibly match the caliber of her own award-winning school orchestra. And a drama class in Henryville! What a joke! After all, her New York teacher boasted professional credits from Off-Broadway and London's West End.

After filling out several forms for the school's office files, Melissa accompanied Mrs. Peters to the music room. She couldn't help but note the physical difference between this school and her beloved Phips Academy in Manhattan, a very exclusive private day school that Melissa attended thanks to the generosity of her California grandparents. They absolutely insisted on contributing to the pricey tuition so that their granddaughter could enjoy the benefits of what many in New York believed to be the finest school in the city. Melissa loved the Phips building with its high ceilings, bell-shaped windows and decorative moldings, marble floors, and the nineteenth-century oil paintings in the social hall. In contrast, Henryville High School was a modern, two-story "horizontal" building with low ceilings, shiny pale green linoleum floors, and plain fluorescent light fixtures. "Except for the couple of student-painted murals on the wall," she thought, "this place is pretty dull."

Melissa was suddenly homesick for Jill and Anna. She remembered that the first rehearsal for *Grease* was scheduled to begin that afternoon. Once more, frustration began to build inside her. Then she heard the music. Melissa's eyes opened wide. She recognized the Strauss waltz. In it were passages that still plagued her. This violinist was note perfect.

Suddenly, Melissa grabbed Mrs. Peters's arm to stop her. "I may not be good enough."

The vice-principal smiled, "You're just a little anxious. That's natural."

But Melissa, who was used to being the best at everything she did, was suddenly not feeling too confident and wouldn't budge. "I didn't bring my violin with me. I'm not prepared." Melissa hoped her nervousness was not obvious to the vice-principal. She tried to sound indifferent.

Mrs. Peters, however, detected the panic in Melissa's voice. "Don't be silly, dear. No one expects you to perform today. I'll just introduce you."

The class bell triggered a sudden explosion of bodies into the hallway. The music teacher was occupied with several other students, so Mrs. Peters decided that Melissa should continue directly to her second period class and pointed her toward the English classroom. Kathy greeted Melissa at the door. "There's an empty seat next to mine," she told her. She took Melissa's hand and guided her inside.

To Melissa's relief, the study of English, French III, and physics did not drastically change fifteen hundred miles inland. But to her dismay, she quickly understood that teachers everywhere love the word "homework." When Melissa walked into the lunchroom, her arms were stacked with books.

"Well, aren't we the studious one," came a voice from behind her. Melissa peeked over her right shoulder and saw Chris's friendly grin.

"I was hoping I'd know someone," she said. "I hate to eat alone."

"Can I give you a hand?" Chris extended his two able arms and Melissa gladly let the books tumble into them. He pretended to look as if the weight of the five textbooks would bring him to his knees. Melissa giggled.

"Did you know your eyes light up when you laugh?" The

boy's voice was quiet and sincere. For just a moment, Melissa wondered if all these weeks she had been fighting destiny. Maybe she was supposed to fall in love with the handsome captain of the high school football team. Then she remembered Tina.

"Anyone else I know eat fifth period?" Melissa started to scan the room for redheads.

"Yeah. Come on over and I'll introduce you to some of the other guys on the team," Chris said. As they approached the table, Johnny McGraw was arm wrestling with another student. Johnny's right shirt sleeve was rolled up almost to his shoulder and his huge, well-defined muscles bulged out from under his skin. Johnny looked up at Melissa and then he announced to his opponent, "Say your prayers, Bowlen. You're going down." With that, Johnny slammed the other boy's hand down on the table. "Want to go for double or nothing?" Johnny challenged. "You could walk out of here twenty bucks richer."

"Oh, no he can't!" a voice shouted, and the entire table looked around at a big, burly man in a rumpled brown sports jacket. His hair was shaved in a crew-cut and Melissa imagined that at one time this man might have been an army drill sergeant.

"Hi there, Coach Kelly," Johnny said sheepishly, his face bright red.

"McGraw, I didn't see exactly what was going on, but I heard something about double or nothing and twenty dollars," the coach said sternly. "You boys know better than to be gambling. Tonight's a big game. We can't afford any suspensions. You understand? Now, whatever you were doing, cut it out."

Not one of the six moved even slightly until the coach had

passed through the cafeteria doors. Johnny broke the silence. "He'd never do it to us," Johnny said. "The coach is a good guy."

"Yeah. But he knows Mrs. Peters would love to put the whole bunch of us through the wringer," said Marty Bowlen, the boy Johnny had just defeated.

"The only one in any wringer is you, my man. You owe me ten big ones," scowled Johnny.

"Wait! I'll take double or nothin'," Marty said. "Meet ya after school. The Sweet Shop."

Johnny looked over toward Melissa. "So, what do you say, Jensen? Should I trust this bozo or do you think he's trying to jew me out of my winnings?"

Melissa flinched. She had never heard that expression, but she understood its offensive reference to Jews as cheats and thieves in business. Her first impulse was to lash out at Johnny, but all eyes were on her. She grew self-conscious. "He looks honest enough to me, McGraw," she said stiffly. "I don't think the question is will he double-cross you and hold onto the money, but can you win again? For all you know, he was hustling you. He went down awfully quickly. I say take the money and run."

"Johnny McGraw don't run from nobody. Anyway, what do you know about gambling?"

Melissa couldn't resist. "I've played a little poker," she remarked coolly.

"Really? Are you challenging me?" The other boys sat there snickering. Even Chris couldn't help but smile.

"Melissa," he whispered at her side, "Johnny is a real card shark. No one can beat him."

"Well," she said with a touch of arrogance, "we'll all have to get together for a friendly game one of these days."

Melissa scooped up her books and went to sit at the next table. Chris immediately followed and took the empty chair next to her. For the rest of the lunch period, Melissa noticed that he paid attention to no one but her. It suddenly dawned on her that this handsome, brawny boy beside her might prove to be just as crude as his pal Johnny. But Chris was so warm and friendly, she refused to believe it.

Her last period was drama and Melissa, much to her dismay, met Johnny again. She was going to ignore him, but he spoke first. "Ain't this a jerky way to end the day?" he sneered. "You won't ever catch me dead on a stage."

"So why are you here?" Melissa asked with disgust.

"I'm here because everybody's got to take one arts elective to graduate this crummy school. Theater didn't sound as awful as glee club or a stupid folk-dancing class. Nah, I got it all figured out. Come the play and I'll hand out programs. Easy 'A.'"

"We do a play?" Melissa brightened.

"Sure. It's a big deal."

The bell rang, and Melissa turned around in her seat. As she did so, she caught a glimpse of another familiar face. He noticed her, too, and smiled. Melissa immediately recognized those powerful eyes. She wanted to introduce herself, but the teacher entered the room and started talking.

Mr. Dennis, her lanky, gray-haired instructor, was lecturing about the Globe Theater in Elizabethan England. Melissa only half listened while she tried to steal glimpses of the boy she had met on the baseball diamond. Several times, he caught her looking at him and smiled. Each time, she blushed. Finally, the bell rang. Everyone bolted toward the door. Melissa grabbed her books and started after the boy with those amazing eyes.

"Miss Jensen, may I have a word with you?" Mr. Dennis stepped in front of her, and the boy disappeared into the hallway.

"Sure, Mr. Dennis."

"I imagine today has been long and a bit overwhelming, so I refrained from making any comments during class. Certainly on your first day, I didn't want to embarrass you," Mr. Dennis said.

Melissa was surprised. "What do you mean?"

"Every time I looked in your direction, you were squirming in your seat. Flirt with the boys on your own time, young lady. Regardless of what you might think, we're a very serious bunch in here. Frankly, from all I had heard about you, I expected much more."

Melissa was tempted to tell this man that his lecture on the Globe was a complete waste of her time, that she had already studied Elizabethan theater last spring, and, in fact, she suspected she could supply several details he had missed. But Melissa knew better than to blurt out her thoughts. After all, she hadn't managed to maintain a 4.0 average most of her school life by insulting teachers. Besides, Mr. Dennis was not just another teacher. He directed the school play. As pathetic as that production might be in this hick town, she knew it was the only acting opportunity she would have this winter. She had no intention of spoiling her chances for a good part, maybe even the lead.

"You're right, Mr. Dennis. It won't happen again," is what she actually said in her most apologetic voice.

"Good. You may go."

Melissa started toward the door, but then stopped. "Johnny said something about a school play?"

"First week in March," the teacher replied. "This whole

year we'll devote to the works of Shakespeare," he told her. "I plan to direct *Romeo and Juliet.*"

"Really? When are tryouts?"

The teacher warmed to her apparent interest. "As a matter of fact, a week from next Tuesday."

"You can be sure you won't catch me squirming in my seat again." Melissa flashed her most engaging smile at Mr. Dennis and then ran out of the room.

Kathy was waiting for her in the hallway. "I love Friday afternoon! Freedom at last!" Kathy exclaimed with glee.

Melissa nodded in full agreement. Although her parents originally suggested that she wait and begin classes on Monday morning, Melissa had insisted that she needed to meet the teachers and get a sense of her workload immediately. That way, she would have the weekend for intense catch-up, if necessary. Her instincts had been correct. Her book bag felt as if she were hauling a ton of bricks.

"Come on. Chris is waiting in the car." Kathy was rushing Melissa, and on their way out the front door, she explained that night's schedule. "My folks will come get you and your parents around 6 P.M. We're having cocktails and hors d'oeuvres at our house. That means cokes and mini pizzas for us," Kathy explained. "Make sure to bring your pajamas and toothbrush for the overnight. Don't worry. We've got a zillion sleeping bags but better bring a pillow. Chris and I have to get back to school early for warm-ups, but my folks will get you to the bleachers by seven-thirty. That's when we start the game. The adults are only staying through half-time. Normally, my folks would stay for the whole game, but this faculty party was planned by the dean's office in honor of your dad. There's no way they can miss it. Don't look so worried. You'll only be by yourself for the second half of the game. Between cheers, I promise to come by and say hello. Who knows? Maybe you'll make some friends in the bleachers." Melissa certainly hoped so.

There was no doubt about it. Henryville High's school spirit was infectious. Time and again that night, Melissa found herself up on her feet cheering with the crowd, which doubly surprised her because in New York she had seldom attended her own school's games. Football had never interested her much. Tonight, however, watching Chris dart across that playing field like a deer in flight was absolutely thrilling. During the second half of the game, Chris leaped into the air and made a breathtaking catch. Melissa could not contain her excitement and automatically turned to the person closest to her. "Unbelievable!" she exclaimed. "Did you see that?"

"That guy's got magic, all right," the boy next to her said. "No one on the other team can even get close to him. I wouldn't be surprised if he goes pro after college." The teenager's eyes gleamed with admiration and just as the words tumbled out of his mouth, Chris scored another touchdown. Melissa screamed wildly.

"Wow! Now, that's what I call school spirit. How come I don't know you? I thought I knew everyone roaming around these 'sacred halls,'" he said.

Introductions followed. Melissa learned that this tall, skinny boy with wire-rimmed glasses and the brown hair was Rob Kingston. She knew why she was sitting all alone at a Friday night football game, but thought it odd anyone else would actually choose to do so.

"My girlfriend, Sharon, was supposed to catch a ride with her uncle from St. Louis. Her family lives there," he explained. "We met through a church youth group. Well, at the last minute, her Uncle Charlie changes his plans and I'm left dateless for the weekend. What can I tell you? I figure, what the hey? I'm not much of a jock but I enjoy football. So I decided I'd hang out at the game." Melissa liked Rob's easy manner and his friendly smile.

Moments after the game, Chris left his jubilant teammates on the field and ran over to Melissa, who was still standing and chatting with Rob in the front row of the bleachers. Chris looked plenty muddy. Beads of perspiration dotted his forehead. In his enthusiasm, Rob stretched out his hand.

"Way to go! Wow! You were like lightning out there." Rob shook Chris's grimy hand with gusto. Then he smiled at Melissa. "Nice talking to you and welcome to the school," he said.

As soon as Rob turned away, Chris asked, "Well, what d'ya think, Melissa?" The football captain was wearing a proud grin. His deep blue eyes sparkled.

"Congratulations!" Melissa's enthusiasm was genuine.

"Hey, you can do better than that." The boy pretended to pout. "For two days, I personally drive you around town and now single-handedly win the game just in your honor. I say all my effort deserves at least a small reward. What do you say?"

Chris jutted out his chin, closed his eyes and puckered his lips. While Melissa inched closer to him and started to lean over the railing, Tina ran up from behind and put her hands around Chris's face. "I'll give you one guess," she squealed. "It's the one who cheered for you the loudest."

Chris turned toward her, and Tina threw her arms around his neck. "My hero," she declared and suddenly kissed him.

Melissa doubted the girl's sincerity because during the embrace Tina's eyes opened and glared up at her. Melissa merely leaned over and pretended to tie her shoelace.

The moment was interrupted when Johnny hollered, "You guys gonna stand there all night? Come on, Chris, we've got to shower and get down to some serious partying." Wiping mud off his forehead, Johnny looked over at Melissa. "So Miss New York City, now ya see how we do it out here. And you can have all that sissy Broadway stuff. Believe me, the plot's always juicier on a football field. Rumor had it we were supposed to lose tonight. Wanna know why? Cause those wimps from North Hills just hired themselves some hot shot Jew as head coach. What a joke! Did they pick themselves a loser or what? I could have told them those people don't know nothin' but how to count money." Johnny laughed maliciously. Tina laughed, too. Melissa's large eyes glared at Johnny with contempt. She was so outraged that she couldn't even get the words out of her mouth. Chris, embarrassed by Johnny's comment, spoke first.

"Hey, Johnny, cool it. We showed those guys who's king. What church they pray at has got nothing to do with it."

In his elated mood, Johnny accepted the chiding graciously—well, graciously for Johnny. "Whatever you say, your royal highness," Johnny said, and he mockingly bowed. Then he bounced up and shouted, "Hey, race ya to the locker room." No sooner were the words out of his mouth than Johnny started sprinting across the field. Chris chased after him, leaving the girls face to face.

"You going to Kathy's?" Tina asked Melissa.

"Yes. You?"

"Nope. Got a date." Tina stuck her nose in the air, turned, and walked away. Melissa was relieved.

"She probably has every right to be jealous," reasoned Melissa. "Frankly, for someone with a girlfriend, Chris is awfully flirtatious." But Melissa made no effort to discourage him. She liked Chris Brown and just couldn't believe he shared Johnny's bigoted notions.

At Kathy's party, the girls spent most of the night talking about their love lives or bemoaning the lack of them. Melissa wasn't surprised that a lot of them had crushes on Chris. But she was still curious about the boy in her drama class and described him to a talkative girl named Jane. "You mean Daniel," Jane said immediately. "You might as well forget him. He's never around on weekends. Leaves every Friday afternoon for Kansas City."

"Why Kansas City? His folks separated?" Melissa thought about her own girlfriend, Jill, who shuttled from parent to parent.

"That's not it," Jane explained.

"So?" Melissa persisted.

The girl leaned over as if to share a confidence. "See, he's the only Jewish kid at school. Personally, I don't care although some people around here don't like him because he's Jewish." Melissa noticed how the girl's eyes scoured the room. "Anyway, on weekends, he hangs out with a whole other crowd. Too bad. He's awfully cute."

Melissa nodded in agreement. On her face was a polite smile. No one could have guessed her discomfort. The rest of the night she carefully observed all these friendly cheerleaders and wondered which ones would automatically hate her once they knew the truth.

4

Daniel

MELISSA DEDICATED THREE HOURS on Saturday and four hours on Sunday to violin practice, and on Monday morning she woke up earlier than usual. She declined Chris's offer for a ride to school. Instead, she asked her mother to take her because she wanted an extra twenty minutes to rehearse alone in the music room.

When Melissa arrived at school, the music room was dark and silent. She flipped the light switch. Melissa's sleepy eyes needed a second to adjust to the bright fluorescent lights overhead. Then she quickly organized her sheet music, adjusted the music stand, and tuned her violin. With her back to the door, she began to perform the piece she had practiced so thoroughly that weekend. It was Brahms's Hungarian Rhapsody. Melissa was so intent on playing with precision as well as with feeling that she heard nothing else but the music.

"Pick up the tempo," a voice suddenly called out to her. Melissa jumped up from her seat. She had no idea that someone was listening from the doorway. It took her only a second to recognize the boy. It was Daniel, the lean, dark, good-looking boy from drama and the baseball field. With his violin already tucked under his chin, he took the seat next to Melissa and began the same musical passage. The richness and clarity of each note as well as his faster pace gave new life to the piece. "See?" he said afterward.

Normally, Melissa would have been insulted. "What arrogance," she would have told Anna and Jill. But she knew immediately that this boy was no show-off. He simply loved playing the violin and his extraordinary technique conveyed that love. She suspected he was the violinist she had overheard Friday morning, the one who had put her into such a frenzy. "You play beautifully," Melissa said with sincere admiration.

"You, too," he answered. With his bow, the boy gently tapped on the sheet music. Melissa understood and raised her violin. Together they filled the room with the Brahms composition. Neither cared that noisy students were slowly meandering into the classroom. Chairs were clanging. Three girls were laughing. Two boys were shouting across the room. Melissa and Daniel heard none of it. For them there was only the Rhapsody. At the bell, the teacher entered. The room fell silent.

Mrs. O'Hara, a petite woman who wore her long snow-white hair wrapped in a bun at the nape of her neck, was not one to waste precious time on formalities. With her reading glasses perched almost at the tip of her nose, she stared down at Melissa. "So you're Miss Jensen. I hope you're ready to work." The teacher turned her gaze to the boy beside

Melissa. "Daniel, make sure our new violinist has a complete copy of our repertoire." Melissa noted that Mrs. O'Hara's manner wasn't mean or harsh. She was just direct and, like all dedicated musicians, very strict. Melissa liked her at once.

For the next forty-five minutes, the group was like any professional orchestra. The musicians were ready and alert, and the conductor waved her baton with absolute authority. Phrases of music were played and replayed to Mrs. O'Hara's satisfaction. Not until the students were packing up their instruments did the teacher's expression relax. "Well," she stated emphatically, "today we made music." She looked over at Melissa. "Glad to have you along."

Melissa beamed. In her wildest dreams, she had never imagined she'd discover such a serious music ensemble. It definitely rivaled hers in New York. And Daniel. Who was this musical prodigy? She walked after him in the hallway. "Excuse me," Melissa said. "Where did you learn to play like that?"

He modestly shrugged. "When I was six years old, my grandmother gave me my first violin. I've been playing ever since."

"Your grandmother teaches you?"

"Not anymore. Now I study at the conservatory in Kansas City," he said.

At lunchtime, Melissa was waiting in the cafeteria line and saw Daniel again. He was sitting alone in the corner. Their eyes met. He waved. She smiled and turned away. Several times she peeked in his direction. He noticed each time. Finally, he approached her. "Didn't your mother ever teach you it's impolite to stare?" he pretended to reprimand her. Melissa became flustered.

"I apologize. Really. I-I'm sorry."

Daniel just laughed. "Hey, I'm only teasing. No need to break out in a cold sweat. After you buy lunch, come on over. I'll give you the rest of the music from Mrs. O'Hara."

As soon as the words were spoken, Rob Kingston stepped between them. "Hey, Daniel, better come with me." Melissa immediately recognized him.

"Well, hi, again," she said in her friendliest voice. "Remember? We met the other night."

Rob gave her a quick glance and nodded hello. He continued tugging at Daniel's arm. "Come on," he urged.

"What's up, Rob?" Daniel asked.

Melissa watched the boys disappear through the cafeteria doors without a word or even a wave. Then she remembered. "Hey! The music!" Melissa exclaimed. She dropped her food tray in the bin and ran out into the hallway. She saw Rob and Daniel turning the corner. They didn't know she was coming up behind them.

"Over there," said Rob. He pointed at a row of lockers. "Go open mine."

Daniel flung open the metal locker door. Melissa saw the words, "JEW LOVER," in glaring red paint, and gasped in horror.

"Who did this?" demanded Daniel. His voice had a slight tremor.

"I don't know but I can guess," Rob said gravely. "I hear comments now and then, but I never thought they'd start messing with my locker. Who knows what they're planning next?"

Out of fear, Melissa blurted out, "You have to report it." Until then, the boys had thought they were alone in the hallway.

"Stay out of this," snapped Daniel. The fear in Daniel's eyes fueled her own. "If you want to help, just keep the locker shut till we get back with some turpentine. Let's check out the art room, Rob."

The paint erased easily. Afterward, Daniel told his friend, "Some stupid moron thinks this is a joke. Please, don't let it get to you."

"Hey, Daniel, you know me," Rob insisted. "I'm cool."

The bell rang. Suddenly the empty hallway was crammed with teenagers. Rob joined the crowd headed downstairs. Melissa and Daniel were still standing by the locker. She refused to budge from the spot. The same outrage she had felt at Johnny's remarks after the football game on Friday night swelled up inside her. Although she was frightened for both of them, she didn't hesitate to speak. "If you know who did it, you've got to tell Mrs. Peters," she insisted.

"Without proof, there's nothing to tell her," Daniel responded with frustration. "Poor Rob. He's such a great guy. Besides being this mathematical whiz, he also happens to be valedictorian of the senior class. The kid's light years ahead of everyone else in this school and not a vicious bone in his body. But some creeps have it in for him because he hangs around with me."

"We have to do something, Daniel," she pleaded. "I know I'm a stranger to Henryville and I have no right to tell you what to do, but—"

"That's right! You are a stranger. You go mouthing off and you'll wake up with swastikas painted all over your sidewalk or something worse. This isn't civics class. This is real life. I advise you not to get involved." Daniel slammed his foot against the locker and walked away from her.

For five minutes, Melissa stood in front of the locker, debating whether or not to go to Mrs. Peters's office. Her feelings kept clouding the issue. She was angry, but she was also scared, and worried that in some cockeyed way, telling Mrs. Peters would be betraying Daniel's trust. Yes, she wanted Daniel to like her but she also knew that she never would have dismissed such a racist act at Phips. Somehow, she would make Daniel understand. Melissa walked to the office and asked to speak with the vice-principal.

"I'm sorry, Melissa," the secretary informed her. "Mrs. Peters is out of the building at an education conference today. Can I help you?"

Melissa shook her head. She decided the vice-principal's absence was an omen. Maybe Mrs. Peters was not the right person. First, she would talk to Anna and Jill or maybe her parents. Suddenly, she wasn't sure what to do but decided she must not act in haste.

After school, Melissa arrived home to an empty house. She found a note on the refrigerator door: "Meetings till after nine. Warm up leftovers. See you tonight. XOXOXOX —M."

Melissa heaved a sigh of frustration. She never liked coming home to an empty house, especially one as gigantic as 189 Willow Lane. It was too early for dinner and still too early to call her girlfriends in New York. Instead, she gobbled down a handful of oatmeal raisin cookies. She then proceeded to spread out her textbooks on the kitchen table. The French grammar assignment went quickly. Physics was another story. She stretched back in the upholstered chair and let out a long yawn. It didn't help. Melissa needed a break. By now at least one of her girlfriends would be home. She walked over to the phone and dialed Anna. No answer. Then she tried Jill. Also no answer. She looked at the clock and seemed confused. "Of course," she suddenly remembered. "It's Monday. Anna and Jill have orchestra."

Melissa returned to the second physics problem. Her mind kept wandering. Try as she might, she couldn't get the locker incident out of her head. Finally, she slammed the book shut. What she needed was exercise. Fresh air would clear her head for the long night ahead. She decided to take a walk and grabbed her jacket.

The cloudy sky was masking the late afternoon sun. The day was gray and the air was damp. Melissa loved the sensation of autumn leaves crunching under her tennis shoes. She strolled over to the campus toward the baseball diamond and saw Daniel jogging around the bases. He waved but kept running. Melissa joined him.

"I'm waiting for Gus," Daniel told her.

"How did you happen to meet him?" she asked, keeping pace with him. She really wanted to talk about the locker, but since he mentioned Gus first, for the moment, she would be patient.

"He's an old friend of my grandparents. In the sixties, he and my grandfather worked together for the Civil Rights Movement. They even knew Martin Luther King."

"Wow!" is all Melissa said. They continued to run around the bases in silence. After two laps, Melissa was feeling too winded to talk about much of anything. Her sides started to ache but she refused to admit fatigue. Finally, Daniel stopped to catch his breath. "You're in pretty good shape," he conceded. He, too, was exhausted but would certainly not be outdone by her. Both flopped down on the grass.

In that next moment, Melissa blurted out what was on her mind. "Aren't you going to do anything at all about what happened today? How can you just forget about it?" she asked.

"No one is forgetting, Melissa, but please, let me handle

this in my own way. I assure you. I have my reasons," he snapped at her.

"Look, you're not the only one affected by racism," she pleaded. "I mean, I'm—"

"Please, Melissa," he earnestly begged her, "I know you mean well and I appreciate it. Really, I do." His tone was considerably softer as his dark expressive eyes stared into her anxious face. "For me, it's not the right time to make it an issue. I'd be very grateful if you would just leave it alone for the moment." He continued to look deep into her eyes.

"I hate to break up such a touching scene, but it's time to play ball, Danny," teased the elderly coach with his distinct, robust belly laugh. Gus had sneaked up behind them. He, of course, had no way of knowing why the boy and girl were staring at one another and just assumed that Cupid was up to his old romantic tricks on a fall afternoon.

"Want to join us, young lady?" Gus asked her.

Any other day, Melissa would have picked up the bat in a second, but at that moment, she preferred to return to her home on Willow Lane. As she walked away, Melissa knew that in order to earn Daniel's trust she would have to remain quiet about the locker. The silence troubled her, but she also liked the fact that they shared a special secret.

Her parents' meeting ran late. By the time they arrived, Melissa was washing up for bed. They wanted to hear all about their daughter's day. She told them about "Mrs. O'Hara's incredible orchestra" and "this sensational violin player named Daniel." However, she never mentioned the locker. She worried they might call the principal. She just couldn't risk losing Daniel's trust.

"Not to change the subject," interrupted her mother, "but I saw Chris's mom and it's all settled. The second weekend in

December we'll have the faculty Christmas party right here in the ballroom. Of course, sweetheart, you can invite some of your new friends from school, so you'll enjoy the party too." As far back as she could remember, Melissa had always invited a few close friends to the family's holiday festivities. Of course, in the last two years, that had included Anna and Jill. Melissa frowned. She knew that in Henryville the one friend she most wanted to invite would have little interest in candy canes.

Like the school orchestra, Melissa's drama class was a surprise. Mr. Dennis had lived in New York for many years, and his résumé included several plays on Broadway as well as roles in some major motion pictures. Melissa was suitably impressed but also puzzled. "How could you give it all up to teach here?" she asked him. After she blurted out her question, she realized Mr. Dennis might be insulted. But the teacher liked her candor.

"I grant you, it's not as glamorous as having your name listed in *Playbill*, but this life has its charm and I no longer have to worry about the top of my head." The teacher chuckled as he patted his receding hair line. Melissa rolled her eyes. "No, really," insisted Tom Dennis. "I enjoy this quiet, easy pace for a change. Besides, the school gives me artistic freedom with a pretty healthy budget to boot. For the first time in my life, I get to choose projects that interest me. Life here can be addicting. I wouldn't be surprised if your parents extended their stay."

Melissa cringed. She had never considered that possibility. Her parents did seem to rave about everything in Henryville. The college faculty was so hospitable. The house was so spacious. They loved the car. They loved their students. They especially loved the adulation.

Of course, they hadn't heard anything about Johnny McGraw. That afternoon, when Mr. Dennis announced the tryouts, Johnny let out a painful groan from his seat. The others laughed. Mr. Dennis ignored it, but at the bell asked both Johnny and Melissa to remain behind. He addressed the boy first.

"I don't appreciate your attitude, Johnny." His words were direct but his manner was still calm. "You may think my class is a joke, but you elected it and I assure you I'm deadly serious about everyone pulling his weight in this class. Got it?"

"Yeah, I got it," Johnny mumbled under his breath. "Anything else?"

The teacher shook his head, and Johnny slammed the door behind him. Secretly, Melissa enjoyed watching Johnny squirm but her face remained expressionless as she waited her turn. She tried to imagine what the teacher wanted. All week she had paid strict attention in class. Melissa had also sized up the competition and calculated she was a strong contender for the lead in the play. Maybe he was ready to offer her the part.

"Melissa," the teacher began, "this past week, I've kept a close eye on you. You've really excelled in our scene study. Very, very impressive."

Melissa could feel her heart pounding inside her chest. Perhaps playing the part of Juliet had been her destiny from the very start. Forget Daniel. She was going to perform the most famous ingenue role in the history of Western theater. She would even apologize to her parents for putting up such a fuss about coming to Henryville. All these thoughts raced through her mind as she smiled up at the director.

"You know you're very gifted," Mr. Dennis continued. "Why, I could cast you with any seasoned professional company. You're ready for the real thing."

"Thank you, Mr. Dennis!" The flattery was much more than Melissa ever expected.

"But you know what I find most commendable?" Melissa shook her head.

"You're a remarkable director. I observed you coaching some of the students during our theater games, and I was quite taken with your ability to convey a concept or a technique. The results were astounding. Have you ever thought of directing?"

Melissa shrugged. "Not really. I like being up on stage too much."

"Well, I want to offer you a new challenge." He paused for Melissa's reaction, but she remained silent. "This year I'd like to try something new. Never done it before. I thought I'd ask my best student to be the assistant director. Shakespeare is so challenging. The actors are going to need a lot of private coaching. After I saw you in class, I figured you're a natural."

"But you haven't heard me read for Juliet. You may change your mind," Melissa said nervously.

"You don't have to worry about an audition for Juliet or any other part," Mr. Dennis said. "Your hard work in class has already earned you the role of my assistant. Besides, I'll expect you to help me cast the show. Your input will be important to me. What do you say? You think you're up to it?"

Melissa stood there dumbfounded. What could she say? All she could do was keep herself from bursting into tears.

"Sure, sounds cool," she said, biting her bottom lip.

5

Auditions

AT TUESDAY'S AUDITION, Melissa sat thoughtfully beside Mr. Dennis. To her credit, she maintained perfect composure. All the while, resentment was building inside her.

"Who's he kidding?" she muttered under her breath. "This guy could care less about my opinions. Assistant director, puh-leeze. All I am is a secretary. For free! What a racket!"

Still, she sat there, conscientiously jotting down the teacher's comments after each reading. For Melissa, it was virtually impossible to watch the other girls with any objectivity. As far as she was concerned, none of them merited the role of Juliet. She decided the least objectionable was Leslie Coles, the flute player in the orchestra. Her eyes did light up once, however.

When Daniel took center stage, he commanded everyone's complete attention in the hall. Afterward, the room rocked with applause. Mr. Dennis leaned over to his assistant director and whispered, "Looks like we found our Romeo."

Melissa heaved a quiet, mournful sigh as she considered one more reason to covet the role of Juliet. Still, she was determined not to dwell on her bad luck. The auditions lasted almost an hour. Afterward, Mr. Dennis quietly matched names to characters. After each decision, Melissa mechanically nodded in agreement. To her, it made no difference. After a few minutes, only one space remained blank. "I'm not sure about Juliet," he told her.

Melissa wanted to run up on stage. "Please, please," she imagined herself begging him, "give me a chance." For a split second, she fantasized about how years later, when she was a famous actress, Mr. Dennis would still be telling his students about this moment of revelation. Of course, it never happened.

"I know who I like," she offered with little enthusiasm.

"Who?" Mr. Dennis asked.

"Leslie."

"Leslie Coles?" The director thought about the choice for a moment. "She's only a sophomore. Leads are always upperclassmen."

"That's stupid," Melissa blurted out a bit too quickly. The teacher looked startled.

"What I mean," she explained in a more conciliatory tone, "is that the choice should be based on talent and dedication, not on someone's grade level. Besides, like Daniel, Leslie is a serious musician. Both she and Daniel understand the demands of rehearsing. Also, she's very pretty and petite, with a fair, creamy complexion. She physically complements Daniel's tall, lean build and olive skin."

Mr. Dennis mulled over the comments for a moment. "You

might have something there. Still, I'm sort of leaning toward Tina Williams. Under the lights, a redhead really dazzles the eye. And her reading was pretty good."

Melissa wondered if her expression matched the disgust churning inside the pit of her stomach. Could her plight get much worse? Not only had she, Melissa Jensen, been denied the opportunity to audition for Juliet, but now the part might be offered to Chris's stuck-up girlfriend. She cautiously paused to consider her response. She knew she must choose each word very carefully.

"What an interesting choice," she began. "I never even considered Tina for the role of Juliet. She just seems a little too, too mature. You know what I mean."

"Well, let me sleep on it tonight," was all the teacher said.

Melissa doubted her arguments had made one bit of difference. When she relayed the episode to her parents, they congratulated her for voicing such a clear and intelligent response. "Big deal," she mumbled. "He's gonna go for Tina. She's gorgeous! Perfect smile. Perfect figure. Perfect skin, hair, and teeth. As long as the girl doesn't open her mouth, she's terrific."

"Was her audition really that horrible?" asked her mother who suspected that her own distraught daughter had abandoned all objectivity.

Truthfully, Melissa could not comment on Tina's audition. During much of it, she had purposefully buried her face in Mr. Dennis's notes. Since that first day in Chris's car, neither girl had very much to say to the other. Of course, the fact that Melissa sat with Chris every afternoon during lunchtime had not gone unnoticed by Tina's girlfriends. After the first day, a lot of people started gossiping. When confronted with the rumor, Melissa shrugged off accusations. In a private moment on the telephone with her friend Jill, however, Melissa had confided the truth. "You know me. I would never intentionally break up any relationship. No matter how cute the guy," she had remarked over the telephone. "But I love the fact Tina feels so threatened. She's such a brat!" Now, thanks to Tom Dennis's partiality to red hair, she might have to deal with this brat on a daily basis. The thought was revolting.

Parts were posted the next morning. A crowd of students hovered around the list. Melissa ignored them all. She just couldn't face Tina's name up there in print. Suddenly, Leslie saw her at the doorway of the music room, pulled her inside, boxed her into a corner of the room, and threw her arms around Melissa's neck. "Thank you," Leslie said, smiling. "A million 'thank yous.' I am so excited. I can't believe it. Mr. Dennis told me you actually suggested it."

"Suggested what?" Melissa asked.

"Me for Juliet. Don't you know? I got the part."

The two girls screamed in unison. Then Melissa squealed, "Leslie, that's terrific!" She was flabbergasted as well as genuinely flattered that Mr. Dennis had listened to her advice. The victory was small, but satisfying.

"You know who Romeo is?" giggled Leslie as she pointed to Daniel, who was tuning his strings across the room.

"Congratulations, Daniel," Melissa called over to him. He immediately stood up and waved.

"Thanks," Daniel said. "When I saw Mr. Dennis this morning, he suggested we get together so you can coach me on lines. He said he's gonna work with Leslie. Is lunchtime good for you?"

Melissa's face radiated with pleasure. Suddenly, the job of assistant director took on a whole new meaning. Why hadn't Mr. Dennis ever mentioned that she would be working individually with Daniel? "Fine with me," she replied happily.

The moment Mrs. O'Hara entered the music room, everyone hushed. For forty-five minutes Melissa played with a new sense of purpose. At the end of the period, Mrs. O'Hara commented, "I don't know what's in the air, young lady, but keep it up."

Melissa was hoping she would have a moment with Daniel after class, but by the time she had packed up her music he had already joined Rob in the hallway. Still pleased with the turn of events, Melissa cheerfully waved to just about everyone she passed in the corridor—even Tina. Regrettably, she also made eye contact with Johnny. "Hey, assistant director," he snidely remarked, "I think your pal Dennis is really losing it." The boy punctuated his nasty remark with an annoying laugh. "Did you see who got the leads?"

Johnny McGraw was the last person in the school Melissa wanted by her side, but the English classroom was just a few steps around the corner. She decided to be polite. "Sure. Leslie and Daniel. What's the problem?" A couple of seconds with Johnny and Melissa's euphoria had fizzled.

"Hey, sweetheart," he said with a crooked smile, "Come on. You know your Shakespeare. We're not doing *Merchant of Venice*. Shylock, yes, but Jew boy playing Romeo? Give me a break. Mr. Dennis needs his head examined."

"Johnny!" She yelled at him. "What's wrong with you?" Her voice oozed with contempt.

"Well, Ex-cuse me! Don't look so pained just because the truth hurts!" he sneered. He grabbed the shoulder of one of his buddies passing in the hall and left Melissa standing there in a silent rage.

When she took her seat by Kathy, Melissa was bristling. "Johnny can be so crude!" Melissa exclaimed.

"Yeah. I guess so," said Kathy, who had no inkling of the conversation. "But even then, he's funny." Kathy's giggle incensed Melissa.

"I don't think so! And what does he have against Daniel?"

"He's Jewish." Kathy shrugged as if it were obvious to the world. Meanwhile, she searched for her mirror and comb inside her purse. "Johnny's whole family hates Jews!" She mentioned this fact nonchalantly as she recurled her bangs.

"Kathy! Don't you think it's wrong?" Totally frustrated, Melissa grabbed the pocket mirror out of Kathy's hand.

"Hey, what d'ya do that for?" Kathy asked. "It's not my fault that bigots live in Henryville. I guess everyone in New York is a saint?" Kathy stuck out her palm and waited for Melissa to return the mirror. "Just thank goodness Tina didn't get chosen for Juliet," Kathy continued.

"Why not?" snapped Melissa, as she grudgingly returned the mirror.

"Well, there would have been fireworks. I mean her father would have had a bird, seeing her opposite Daniel. I once heard him on this call-in radio show. He says the reason our country is in such a mess is because rich Jews in Hollywood control all the money. He says they 'buy' the politicians and keep them in their back pockets."

"Kathy, you don't believe that nonsense!"

"Nah," Kathy answered with conviction, and Melissa breathed a quiet sigh of relief. "I don't even care about politics," Kathy added as she slipped her comb and mirror back into her pocketbook.

Melissa didn't know which was more troubling—Johnny's prejudice or Kathy's indifference. At lunchtime, she was glad to spend the time with Daniel.

"Hi," he greeted her. The handsome boy stood up, holding

his script opened to page one. Melissa found herself staring at his long, jet-black eyelashes.

"Something wrong?" he asked.

Melissa snapped out of her trance. "Sorry," she said with an embarrassed giggle. "You ready to rehearse?" she asked as she sat down at the lunch table.

"Not on an empty stomach," Daniel said.

"All right," said Melissa, bouncing up to get into the long cafeteria line. "Let's get something to eat."

"You go ahead. I brought mine from home." Daniel held up his brown paper bag. "My grandmother packs enough food for a week. Want to share?"

Melissa smiled and sat down again. Since she had met him, Daniel had not shown her this much attention.

She had to chuckle as he unpacked his lunch. Most items had been carefully wrapped in aluminum foil and then covered with plastic wrap.

"My grandmother must know yours," Melissa laughed. "She packs leftovers the exact same way. I take it yours lives with you?"

"More like I live with her," Daniel replied. "My dad's company transferred him to Tokyo for two years. My mom teaches piano at the college, but they gave her a sabbatical so she could go too."

"How 'bout you? I think Japan sounds exciting."

Daniel glanced around the lunchroom. "It's not like I have any great love for this place, but I've less than a year to graduation. It seemed easier to stay put. Besides, I've got a phenomenal teacher at the Conservatory. With his help and a little luck, I may have a shot at Julliard."

"Definitely," declared Melissa, who had no doubt that Daniel was destined for a brilliant career.

Her certainty embarrassed Daniel. He lowered his eyes and shrugged. "We'll see." After an awkward pause, he remembered lunch. "Hey, let's see what Grandma packed today," Daniel said.

The lunch was pretty typical. One tuna salad and one cheese sandwich, an apple, one miniature box of raisins, and a small bag of chips. Dessert was a real treat. Daniel unwrapped two large cherry hamantaschen. Melissa took a big bite of the fruit-filled doughy pastry and smacked her lips. "Mm. Delicious," she squealed.

"Betcha don't know what these cakes are called," teased Daniel.

"Betcha I do," said Melissa. "Hamantaschen!" Daniel's eyes opened in amazement. "Don't look so shocked," Melissa said. "Almost every bakery in New York sells them. But not as good as this." She licked her lips once more.

"Of course not. My grandmother is the finest baker anywhere. My grandpa used to brag to everyone. Hamantaschen were his favorite." Suddenly his eyes looked sad. His voice softened. "My grandfather died last May. Sudden heart attack." He sighed and thought for a moment. "I have this theory. Whenever Grandma is missing him most, she whips up a batch of hamantaschen. Believe me, I've eaten a lot since I moved in with her. Not that I'm complaining."

He took another bite and then a glint of mischief sparkled in his eyes. "OK smarty-pants," Daniel said. "You knew the name. But what's the origin of hamantaschen?"

Melissa shrugged. Somehow, she remembered a Jewish holiday that began with the letter "P." She also remembered going to synagogue and turning noise-makers. But that was when she had been very young. At the moment, the only holiday she could think of was Passover. She knew that wasn't right.

"There's a holiday called Purim," Daniel explained. "Usually comes anywhere from late February to mid-March. Anyway, it celebrates the Jewish people's triumph in Persia over an evil man named Haman who tried to destroy the Jews like Hitler in World War II. The day the Jews were to be struck down, Haman swung from the gallows instead."

"But why hamantaschen?" asked Melissa as she popped another chunk into her mouth. Daniel pointed to what was left of his triangular cake and, with his index finger, outlined the three sides.

"Haman was supposed to have worn a three-cornered hat. See?"

"Sure," said Melissa.

"So now, every year at Purim, Jews around the world bake hamantaschen to remember their victory over Haman. But none are as delicious as my grandmother's," he announced proudly.

"She sounds like a very special woman," replied Melissa warmly.

Daniel grinned. "She's one of a kind," he said with genuine pride and slight amusement. "Of course, this last month she hasn't felt too well. Asthma." He looked serious again. "That's why I didn't make an issue about the locker. My parents are halfway around the world, and my grandmother doesn't need any stress in her life right now."

"I didn't tell anyone," Melissa reassured him. She was still uneasy about her decision, but now, more than ever, she did not want to do anything to put a damper on their budding friendship. When he asked her about Sunday, she knew she had made the right choice.

"How about if early Sunday night when I get back from the Conservatory, you come over? We'll work on lines and you can meet Grandma. Give me your address and phone number. I'll call as soon as I'm back in town."

Melissa hurriedly wrote down the information. She didn't want to appear too eager, but her stomach fluttered with excitement and her heart felt as if it were thumping double-time. As she handed him the scrap of notebook paper, Melissa marveled at life's little surprises. Yesterday, she would have liked to tar and feather Mr. Dennis. Now, suddenly, he was Melissa's hero. If not for him, Daniel might never have given her a second glance. When Daniel confessed that he had never actually read *Romeo and Juliet*, Melissa insisted that they begin reading the play immediately. Melissa had just studied the tragic drama in her literature class last spring and absolutely adored the story. Her enthusiasm made Daniel even more determined to tackle the strange language. They were just finishing Act I when the bell rang. Daniel jumped to his feet.

"Sorry, Melissa, but I've got to rush to chemistry lab. I'll finish reading the play tonight so we can talk about it more tomorrow. I really appreciate your help." He grabbed the script, threw it in his knapsack, and turned toward the door.

"Listen," Melissa called after him, "if while you're reading you have any questions, jot 'em down and we'll talk tomorrow."

"Or even better, I'll just pick up the telephone tonight." He held up the sheet with her telephone number and grinned. His smile made Melissa's stomach start to flutter all over again. She watched him exit out the door and stood up to pick up her own stack of books.

"I missed you at our table." The voice startled Melissa and she turned abruptly. She hadn't realized Chris was beside her.

"Hi, Chris," she said.

"What were you doing over here with Daniel?" he asked.

"Don't you know?" Melissa looked surprised. "I'm the assistant director of the school play. Mr. Dennis thought Daniel should get an early start memorizing his lines. Believe me, Shakespeare is really tough. I'm supposed to coach him. And well, lunch seemed as good a time as any. You want to start walking to class? I'm just down the hall."

Chris didn't budge. He stood there, blocking her path so she couldn't get to the door. "I think that's great about you being assistant director," he said. "Although I say Mr. Dennis missed the boat when he didn't make you Juliet."

Melissa couldn't help but smile at the compliment. She wondered why he wouldn't have preferred Tina but didn't ask. "Thanks. What can I say?" With a dramatic heave of the shoulders, she said, "You win some. You lose some. That's show biz."

"Well, I'm gonna set old Johnny straight," Chris suddenly grumbled.

"What do you mean?" Melissa asked.

"He saw you two over here and he started razzin' me. I told him I thought you were just doing something for school, but you know Johnny. He's got a grudge against Daniel because he's Jewish. I think that's pretty stupid, myself, because Daniel's a good guy. We go back a long way. Since grade school. I really wish Johnny would ease up. But I will admit, I was a little curious about what you two were doing. The other guys all thought you looked real cozy."

"Wait a minute! No one was *cozy* here. We were rehearsing!" Melissa's nostrils flared and her cheeks turned a flaming red. Chris suddenly flashed one of his dimpled smiles, which only incensed her more. "Why are you grinning at me?" she snapped.

"I can't help it," Chris replied. "Even when you're angry, you're great looking. Your skin gets like a rose color. Hey, listen, I was wrong. I had no right to question you. Come on. We're both going to be late for class."

Melissa was indeed three minutes late for French class, and Monsieur Hobart was not especially understanding. "Mademoiselle Jensen, punctuality is an indicator of a student's attitude. One can not be an 'A' student if one simply shuffles in and out of class whenever it suits her fancy. Comprenez-vous?" Melissa understood very well. After all, she had a reputation to uphold. During her entire academic career, she had maintained only excellent grades in New York City. If her averages slipped, how could she ever face those teachers back home who had given her such glowing reports? She silently vowed to stop being so easily distracted by her infatuation with Daniel, Chris's flirtations, and even awful Johnny. She would concentrate fully on her studies.

The oath lasted until nine-thirty in the evening. With her homework completed, she began to wonder about a phone call from Daniel. But the phone never rang.

6

Sunday

ON THAT COLD SUNDAY morning before Thanksgiving, Melissa, bundled in her quilted bathrobe, sat by the kitchen telephone talking to her grandmother in New York City. She didn't care that her mother stood only several feet from her, beating eggs at the counter and listening to every word. "So anyway, Grandma," Melissa was explaining, "he already plays like a concert violinist. He's unbelievable. I'm sure he's going to be very famous one day. Right now, he studies at the conservatory in Kansas City. His name? Daniel. Daniel Goodman." After she hung up, Melissa turned to her mom. "Grandma sends her love. She didn't want to disturb you while you were making breakfast. She says she'll call back tonight."

Melissa's mother gave her daughter a quizzical look. "So tell me more about this Daniel. I remember you mentioning a talented violinist."

"I was going to tell you and Daddy at breakfast. Daniel plays Romeo. He's the one I coach."

Mrs. Jensen smiled. "Somehow I suspect that this Romeo was the reason you decided assistant director isn't such an awful job."

"Puh-leeze, Mother. Don't make a big deal out of it. I'm his coach. That's all."

Melissa's mother was still puzzled. "It's so unlike you to mention anything about your social life to your grandmother. I mean I know she lectures you."

"True. But I knew she would approve of Daniel," Melissa said. "He's Jewish."

"Who's Jewish?" asked Michael Jensen as he groggily entered the kitchen, shuffling along in his slippers and terrycloth robe. His face lit up with a smile of satisfaction as he inhaled the aroma of his wife's freshly brewed coffee.

Without having to be asked, Melissa reached for a coffee cup from the cupboard. As she handed her father his mug, Melissa started to tell both her parents about Daniel—how they first met on the baseball field and then in orchestra class. She explained that his own folks were away in Japan and that he lived with his grandmother. "In fact, I promised Daniel I'd go over there and rehearse with him later," Melissa said.

"Why didn't you say something earlier?" Her mother's voice sounded uncharacteristically shrill. "I told you I invited the Browns over for the afternoon. You knew Chris and Kathy were coming."

Melissa held her hands up in defense. "Mom, don't get so excited. Daniel won't be home from his violin lesson till five or six. We're rehearsing at his grandmother's house tonight."

Satisfied, Melissa's mother prepared French toast and no

one mentioned Daniel again. Instead, Anita explained everyone's household duties in preparation for their afternoon
guests.

After a leisurely breakfast, Melissa's father disappeared into
the living room and, after a few futile attempts, proudly
produced a crackling fire in the grand marble fireplace.
Meanwhile, Melissa washed the dirty breakfast dishes while
her mother set up the luncheon buffet on the mahogany
dining table. Afterward, all hurried upstairs to shower and
dress.

The doorbell rang at 1 P.M. sharp. Melissa checked her hair
one last time in her mirror. From the upstairs window, she
peeked through the lace curtain and saw the familiar station
wagon parked in front of the house. She was running down
the steps as her parents opened the door. Chris, Kathy, and
Mr. and Mrs. Brown all entered with their arms loaded with
boxes. "Oh, Anita, dear, I do hope you don't mind, but since
we were all coming together, it just made more sense to bring
the holiday decorations now. I know I'm a bit early."

"Like four weeks," Kathy muttered sarcastically.

Mrs. Brown's eyes flashed her daughter a silent reprimand.
Then she turned to her hostess. "I hope you won't mind
storing them. It just seemed so convenient."

Her mother shook her short, red curls and smiled graciously. "Don't be silly. Let's see what we have."

One by one, Mrs. Brown lovingly showed off her collection
of ornaments. Within moments the foyer was lined with
hand-painted angels, crystal bells, ceramic gingerbread men,
wooden soldiers, Santa Clauses and reindeer designed in
petit point, and shiny silver stars. With each ornament came
a special story. Melissa listened respectfully, but privately she
felt odd about the whole scene. Did the Browns even know

they were Jewish? She was relieved when the last elf was finally unpacked, and her mother insisted they eat. "Let's not bother rewrapping all this stuff now," said Melissa's mother. "I have sandwiches and salad set up in the other room." At the first mention of food, the three teenagers eagerly adjourned to the dining room.

Afterward, when the adults congregated in the living room, Melissa took Kathy and Chris into her father's study. Of all the rooms in the big house, Melissa decided she liked the study best, with its wall-to-wall bookshelves, massive oak antique desk, and "butter soft" burgundy leather sofa. She had even taken the liberty of setting up her music stand in the corner, and whenever the space was vacant Melissa took possession. Upon entering, the two girls curled up on either end of the couch, but Chris sat down on the carpet with his back against the front of the hand-carved desk. Kathy was her usual chatty, bubbly self, but Chris seemed a bit distracted. When Tina's name came up in conversation, Chris suddenly excused himself to make a phone call in the kitchen.

Kathy huddled closer to Melissa. "I know a secret," she taunted.

"What?" Melissa asked.

"It's about Tina." She stuck out her tongue and made an unflattering face. Melissa laughed.

"So?"

"It's over," Kathy declared.

"What's over?" Melissa looked confused.

"Their relationship or whatever you want to call it," Kathy replied. "I knew it was coming sooner or later. Thanks to you, it's sooner!"

"Hey, what do you mean, thanks to me?"

"Listen, Tina was always whining about something, but

since you showed up they've been fighting nonstop."

"Really?" Melissa lowered her green eyes. Looking down at the sofa cushion, she suddenly felt very guilty. She liked Daniel and had never intended to give Chris the wrong impression. "Don't sweat it. I'm thrilled." Kathy gave Melissa a big squeeze and whispered in her ear, "So is someone else, but that's for him to tell you. I'm probably going to get shot for opening my big trap."

A few moments later, Chris returned to the study. He said nothing about his phone call, but Melissa noticed he seemed more relaxed. After a while, he began to entertain the two girls with his imitations of several of the teachers. "You've got a terrific ear," Melissa squealed between her fits of laughter. That single statement was all the encouragement Chris needed. For the next hour, he performed for Melissa and his sister, doing pratfalls, telling jokes—even performing a couple of magic tricks.

Later, while Kathy and her parents were standing in the doorway saying their thank yous, Chris insisted that Melissa walk him down to the car. "Everyone will be gossiping tomorrow, so you might as well hear my side of the story," he began sheepishly. "I broke up with Tina. It would have happened eventually. She's just too possessive. I still feel awfully bad. I didn't want to hurt her but I've got a life, too."

For a couple seconds, Chris looked uncharacteristically thoughtful. His seriousness made Melissa uneasy. She suspected Chris's decision had been motivated by his feelings for her. Why couldn't it be Daniel's dark, captivating eyes looking at her so tenderly? Chris's affections only served as a reminder that she had not told him or anyone else in Henryville that she was Jewish. "But Chris will not be the first I tell," she decided. "First, I tell Daniel."

After their guests left, Melissa joined her parents in the living room. Melissa's dad was adding another log to the roaring fire. She picked up a handful of pretzel wheels from the bowl on the coffee table and flopped down into the easy chair to enjoy the warmth of the fireplace. She started munching on the crunchy snack.

"Chris's dad mentioned something that's sort of troubling." Her father's tone prompted Melissa to sit up and stop eating. "When I took this job, I never considered it a potential problem. But come to think about it, I have read about such things popping up on college campuses." He paused. "This morning, one of the theater teachers stopped at her office to pick up a textbook," he explained. "On her desk, she noticed a newsletter."

"So, what's the big deal?" Melissa popped another tiny pretzel into her mouth. She hated it when her father "over-dramatized."

"It was anti-Semitic propaganda. This teacher, by the way, isn't Jewish. But her new husband just happens to be named Steinberg."

Melissa stopped munching and her expression turned serious.

"No need to worry, Melissa," her mother assured her. "After all, this isn't Nazi Germany. We're Americans!"

Melissa remained thoughtful. "But, we're Jewish, too," she answered both her parents.

"And haven't your mother and I always taught you to be proud of who you are?" Melissa heard her father's voice rise another decibel.

"Dad, take it easy. I didn't mean to upset you. It just seems that our being Jewish is something you'd rather not make public."

"It's not like that at all," he contradicted her. Melissa recognized the defensive tone. He had used it often around her grandparents in New York. "I've never denied the fact that I was born Jewish," he insisted. "It just seems ludicrous that I should be discriminated against for a religion I barely practice. It's my decision. Simple as that."

As Melissa grabbed another handful of pretzels, she wondered whether Johnny McGraw and his kind really allowed any of them that simple a choice. Of course, she couldn't mention Johnny without betraying Daniel. So she said nothing.

Daniel arrived at six-thirty. Melissa was ready and waiting in her red ski jacket and mittens. She always felt so awkward introducing new boys to her parents, but, of course, they were standing by the door waiting eagerly.

"Very nice to meet you, Mr. Jensen," Daniel said politely and extended his hand. As Daniel greeted her mother, Melissa suddenly realized how the foyer must look to him. All the Christmas ornaments were still unwrapped. In her total embarrassment, she tried to sound as natural as possible.

"Please excuse the mess," she apologized. "As you can see, my mom's planning ahead—decorations for the college's faculty party in December."

"Michael," her mother said. "We've got to get everything boxed tonight before there's an accident. I'd feel terrible if anything happened to these lovely family heirlooms."

"Of course, sweetheart. As soon as the kids are on their way." Then he turned to Daniel. "Now, Daniel, you must come back in December," Melissa's dad told him. "This old house is going to make a fabulous setting for our party."

Melissa understood perfectly that her father was referring

to the Christmas party for the college, but in front of Daniel it all seemed so awkward. Luckily, he simply smiled and promised to have Melissa back by nine-thirty.

Driving up to the house in the dark, Melissa could not fully appreciate the pastoral beauty surrounding Mrs. Goodman's stone cottage on the outskirts of Henryville. Daniel told her the small house sat on two acres of land dotted with oak and pine trees. In the summer, beds of wild flowers, a prize-winning rose garden, and an elaborate vegetable patch were his grandmother's pride and joy. Certainly, the setting was completely different from Melissa's own grandparents' New York apartment. Still, as she stood at the front door, the outside porch light shone on a mezuzzah attached to the door post. She looked up at it. She knew her grandparents had one on the door-post of their apartment in New York. Daniel noticed her staring up at the mezuzzah. "In there is one of the most important prayers in the Jewish religion," Daniel told her as he gently touched it. "It is called the *Shema*. In the prayer we acknowledge there is only one God."

Melissa nodded and was about to tell him that her grandparents also had a mezuzzah on their doorpost when the front door suddenly opened wide. Still in her striped apron and patting her wet hands on the pockets, Mrs. Goodman greeted Melissa. She was a small woman with thick, wavy white hair, delicate features, and a warm smile.

"Daniel has that smile," Melissa noted to herself. Mrs. Goodman didn't look ill, but Melissa heard her wheeze with each breath.

"Come in. Come in. Oy, such a pretty girl and Daniel tells me you also play the violin. Sometime, you two must give a concert." Daniel's eyes expressed his disapproval. "Oy, I know that look, Daniel. That look your grandfather would give me when he wanted me to stop talking so much."

"I've heard a lot about you, Mrs. Goodman," said Melissa, who saw much of her own grandmother's manner in the elderly woman.

"Look, I promise to leave you children alone to work, but first, I insist you join me for strudel." She pointed to the tiny dining area, and both youngsters obediently took their places at the table.

Mrs. Goodman had taken great care to set the table with pretty floral teacups and matching dessert dishes. In the center stood two old-fashioned brass candlesticks.

Without even thinking, Melissa commented, "My grandmother in New York has a pair that's almost identical."

Mrs. Goodman's face beamed. "These candlesticks were my mother's. I light them every Friday night. One day, when Daniel has his own family, it will be my pleasure to give them to his wife—whoever that lucky girl may be."

The elderly woman looked lovingly at her grandson, but the self-conscious teenager's expression indicated that she was again talking too much. Mrs. Goodman changed the subject. "Daniel tells me your father's in the theater?"

"He's a playwright," Melissa said.

Mrs. Goodman's mouth suddenly dropped open. "Oy! I know who he is. Of course. Michael Jensen." Melissa nodded. "I've seen plays of his at the dinner theater in Kansas City. Vey es mire! Wait till my ladies in the bridge club hear this one."

Melissa was always very happy when one of her parents' names was recognized. "He's working on a play at the college that might even go to Broadway," she bragged.

"Really?" said Daniel. He looked and sounded genuinely impressed.

"Well, I'm waiting to hear my Daniel play at Carnegie Hall," Mrs. Goodman announced.

"Grandma!" groaned Daniel. "Stop embarrassing me."

"Oy, everything embarrasses you." The boy shook his head in silence as he popped the last bite of pastry into his mouth. "OK, OK, I promise I won't say another word." Mrs. Goodman removed the three sticky dessert dishes and disappeared into the kitchen.

Daniel opened his script to the balcony scene. "Let's start here," he insisted.

The first couple of times, they merely read the lines. Then Melissa took his script. "OK," she said. "Let's see what you know, and remember, make each moment fresh and spontaneous. Don't anticipate the outcome. I'll try to surprise you and you surprise me."

Melissa could tell from the start that Daniel was a natural actor. It never seemed like he was playing a role, but more like he was Romeo. Of course, Melissa proved to be his equal and a captivating Juliet. Before long, the two became so absorbed in their work they didn't realize that Mrs. Goodman was standing in the back corner of the room. At the closing line, she applauded.

"That was outstanding! Melissa, it's a shanda that you're not playing Juliet. You were born to play that part!"

"Thank you Mrs. Goodman," Melissa said with sincere appreciation, "but I'm only the assistant director."

"Not *only*," Daniel insisted. "Without you, I wouldn't even understand this play."

"You know, I told Daniel before you came how much I always loved this story. On one of my first dates with Daniel's grandfather, we went to see a production in downtown Kansas City. Brings back memories." Mrs. Goodman paused as she sighed with nostalgia. "But tonight, listening to the lines again, it reminded me of a wonderful story I've been telling Daniel since he was a little boy."

Daniel groaned. "Oh, not that one again, Grandma!"

"Well, it is an old Jewish legend."

"What is it?" demanded Melissa.

Mrs. Goodman's face lit up with pleasure. "They say that when a soul descends from Heaven, that soul contains both male and female elements: the male part enters one baby and the female another."

Melissa looked puzzled. "I don't get it, Mrs. Goodman. What's the connection to *Romeo and Juliet?*"

"Ah," exclaimed the grandmother. "It is believed that if the two youngsters prove themselves worthy, both parts of the soul will reunite in marriage."

In her moment of revelation, Melissa gushed, "How romantic!"

Daniel rolled his eyes and his grandmother chuckled.

"There's a good reason this play has lasted so long, even when people are skeptics like you, darling," and she patted her grandson on his broad shoulder. "Like it or not, love controls our destiny. That's because there is a divine plan." Mrs. Goodman gave Melissa a warm smile and quietly returned to the kitchen.

The rehearsal continued for another fifty minutes. Every so often, Melissa would stop to offer a suggestion. It all felt so comfortable that, in his excitement, Daniel grabbed Melissa by the shoulders. "You're fantastic," he said with genuine admiration. His face inched closer. Their eyes locked. She remained very still and waited for his lips to meet hers. Suddenly, Daniel turned from her.

"Sorry," he said nervously.

In the next moment, he went to get their coats. Melissa made no comment, except to tell Mrs. Goodman how much she had liked her strudel and story and hoped to see her again soon.

The ride back to Willow Lane was awkward for both of them. As much as Melissa tried to keep the conversation upbeat, Daniel seemed tired and not very talkative. She didn't understand what was wrong. Had she done something to offend him? But what? She figured when they arrived at her house, he would walk her up to the door, and that would be the perfect time to tell him she was Jewish. Maybe he'd even come inside for a while. Her mom had bought marshmallows. They could have hot cocoa in the kitchen. As all this was running through her head, Daniel pulled the car up to the curb. She waited. "See ya tomorrow. I've got to get back," is all he said. He turned his eyes away from her and looked ahead into the dark.

Melissa got the hint. She slammed the car door and ran up the front steps in a huff. How rude of him to just drop her off like that. It seemed he couldn't get rid of her quickly enough. As she closed the front door behind her, she heard the phone ring.

"Is that you, Melissa?" her father called out from his study. "Chris is on the line. It's the third time he's called tonight."

7

The Winter Concert

THE NEXT DAY, when Melissa walked over to Daniel in the cafeteria, he stunned her before she could even unload her books. "Thanks for last night," he informed her, "but you don't have to help me anymore. Mr. Dennis and I both agree you should be coaching Leslie."

"Why can't I help both of you?"

Daniel shook his head. "Really, it's not necessary. If I have a problem, I'll ask Mr. Dennis." His manner and tone made it apparent that he did not want her company. Melissa merely nodded and turned to find Leslie.

From then on, Melissa and Leslie devoted their every spare moment to the play. In the process, the girls became close friends, and Melissa soon acknowledged her own frustration and disappointment that Daniel had rejected her as his coach.

"His loss. My gain," Leslie had replied warmly.

It was then Melissa revealed her secret about the locker. "But you can never tell anyone," Melissa begged Leslie.

"You know it was Johnny!" Leslie pronounced with disgust upon hearing the ugly locker story. "Poor Daniel. He must feel like everyone hates him."

"Well, an incident like that would make a person paranoid," admitted Melissa. "I mean it certainly scared me!"

"Why should it scare you? Only someone Jewish—" The flute player stopped in midsentence.

Melissa quietly acknowledged her friend's suspicion. "The crazy thing is that when I lived in New York, being Jewish never mattered to me! But here, I think about it all the time. Unfortunately, so do a lot of other people."

"We're not all like Johnny," Leslie assured her.

Despite their best intentions, neither Jill nor Anna could visit during the holiday break from classes. Still, Melissa wasn't too disappointed because she had Leslie. Almost every afternoon, the girls found their way to Sarah's Sweet Shop, where they gossiped over some gooey ice cream delight. The afternoon before New Year's Eve, they sat in their regular booth by the parking lot window.

"Look out there," Leslie whispered as she licked the last drop of fudge from her spoon. "It's Johnny and his dad getting out of that green truck."

Melissa peered through the window. "Wow! He's even bigger than Johnny!" She couldn't help but notice how the father's frame dwarfed even Johnny's powerful build. The two appeared to be alone in the parking lot in the middle of a heated discussion. To the girls' horror, they watched Jim McGraw grab his son suddenly by the jacket collar and slam Johnny's body against the side of the pick-up truck. Afterward, the girls saw Johnny limping after his father.

Leslie leaned toward Melissa. "They say when he's drinking, he gets real violent. I guess Jim McGraw started celebrating New Year's a bit early."

"Where's Johnny's mother?" Melissa asked.

"No one knows."

"But Johnny shouldn't be living with him," Melissa asserted.

"Are you kidding?" mocked Leslie. "To hear Johnny talk, you would think his father is a god. I have this theory. Johnny's crude because of his miserable home life. He does and says such awful things for shock effect—just to get attention. My mom always says, 'Can't learn to love if never been loved.'" Leslie paused to consider the phrase. "It's pretty sad," she sighed.

"Even sadder," Melissa thought to herself, "is that Chris and everyone else tolerate him."

It was New Year's Day, and at noontime Melissa was still curled up in bed. She was wide awake but wanted to stay warm under her fluffy goose-feathered quilt, a special gift from her grandmother. The quilt dated back to the turn of the century, when her grandmother's grandmother had received it as a wedding present in Salzburg, Austria. Whenever Melissa had stayed overnight during the winter at her grandparents' apartment, she had looked forward to wrapping herself in this luxurious comforter. Her mother had repeatedly protested that the quilt was just too bulky to pack up for Henryville, but her grandmother had insisted and finally prevailed—and thank goodness for that. The big stone house in the middle of Rich Man's Alley was incredibly charming, but its insulation was anything but ideal. These winter nights when the wind howled at her window, Melissa snuggled under that quilt and silently praised her grand-mother for her generosity and persistence. When Melissa finally decided to make her grand entrance, she flopped down the stairs in her old flannel bathrobe and her very worn purple and green furry slippers. The old shoes made her long, graceful feet look more like two walking eggplants. She strolled into her father's study and gently kissed him on the cheek. He looked up from his journal. "And Happy New Year to you too," he said cheerfully. "Your mother and I thought you might miss the whole day, sleepy head. You didn't even hear the telephone ring."

"Oh, who called?"

"Well, while you were enjoying your beauty rest, your mom and I went out for a jog. We came back and found these messages on the answering machine. Might want to hear them." Michael Jensen pushed the replay button.

"Hi, Melissa! It's Tom Dennis. Well, do I have a New Year's surprise for you! Call me at 538-7690."

A couple of moments later, she heard Leslie's voice: "Mel, it's Leslie. The most unbelievable thing has happened. I received a music scholarship to study with this phenomenal flute teacher at a high school outside Boston. I can't wait to tell you all the details. But listen to this! Mr. Dennis wants you to play Juliet."

Melissa called Leslie first.

"What do you mean I'm playing Juliet? You never even mentioned Boston. Why can't you start this school next September?" Melissa was pleading with Leslie. In the last month, she knew just how hard Leslie had worked on her part. Besides, Leslie had become her one true friend in Henryville. As much as she wanted to be Juliet, Melissa dreaded the thought of facing the next five months alone.

"Are you kidding?" Leslie said with disbelief. "This is a chance of a lifetime. I never said anything because it was such a long shot. Actually, I was number three on the list. The student they awarded the scholarship to had to drop out. Don't ask me why. Then the kid they chose before me just came down with mononucleosis. Tough break for him. The doctors figure anywhere from six weeks to three months. So fortune has smiled on an unknown flute player from Henryville, Missouri. The money's available and has to be used this semester. Can you believe it? I'm sorry I didn't tell you earlier. Really, I am. I got the call before Christmas, but my folks wouldn't let me breathe a word of it to anyone until I had a chance to talk to Mr. Dennis. Well, he spent the holiday skiing in Colorado. Every day I've been dying to tell you. I finally got him on the telephone this morning. I told Mr. Dennis you know the role backwards. He thinks it's a great idea for you to step in as Juliet. Mel, the way I see it, you were always meant to be the star. Who knows? Maybe this is fate's way of finally bringing you and Daniel together."

Leslie was giggling, but Melissa took the comment to heart.

After winter break, Leslie returned to school for one last week. On the day of Leslie's departure, Melissa felt more alone than when she had first arrived in Henryville. She noticed Daniel reading alone at his corner table in the cafeteria. She walked over to him and cleared her throat. "Hi!" she said trying to sound cheerful. "I thought maybe since we're going to be working on stage together, you might like to get in a little extra rehearsal during lunch. I sure could use the help."

"Who, you? You're fabulous," he assured her. "But right now, I've got to get back to this book. I've got a report due sixth period," he answered and flipped to the next page of Dickens' *A Tale of Two Cities.*

Melissa was still wandering around the cafeteria, looking for someone to sit with, when Chris approached her. "You look like a lost puppy," he teased her good-naturedly. "Come on over and join the gang."

"No," is all she said.

"Well, then, I'll come sit with you," Chris offered.

After the rejection from Daniel, it was hard to resist Chris's warm, friendly smile. She followed him to an empty table. Since his break-up with Tina, Melissa had known Chris wanted to date her. He telephoned a lot, but she didn't care for him in the same way and, so far, had tactfully avoided him. In the last month, her rehearsals with Leslie had been a convenient excuse not to join him at lunchtime, and in the mornings she insisted that one of her parents drive her to school.

"It's great about you getting the role of Juliet," he began. "I always thought that's how it should have been from the start."

A strand of Melissa's blond hair fell over her eyes. Gently, Chris brushed it away from her forehead. She blushed.

"Look," Chris continued, "I have a confession. I'm jealous of Daniel. He's gonna spend all that time with you rehearsing on stage. What do you say? Can't you squeeze me in anywhere? Please?" His charming persistence made her laugh.

"It could never work out," she said quietly.

"It's Johnny, isn't it?" he asked in an angry whisper. "I watch you cringe every time he makes those ethnic jokes. I've told him to stop, but he just doesn't get it. Why blame me for his rudeness?"

Melissa's green eyes flared with anger. "He's your friend, which leaves me out of the picture," she snapped at him. "See, like Daniel, I'm Jewish." It felt good to tell Chris the truth. She only regretted that she still hadn't told Daniel.

It took Chris a moment to absorb the impact of her statement. "You never said anything. Not that it matters to me," he added quickly. "From the first day we met at the airport, I've really liked you. Do you think I'm prejudiced, too?"

"I don't know what to think," Melissa groaned.

"Well, me neither," Chris snapped back at her.

"What do you mean?"

"You have a funny way of being Jewish. I mean, hosting a Christmas party is kind of strange. At least with Daniel, you know where he stands. What kind of Jews are you, anyway?" Chris stood up and turned abruptly.

Melissa jumped up and called after him. "Chris! Please wait!" She grabbed him by the shoulder and was surprised when he looked at her with such a solemn expression and placed his hand on top of hers. His voice was low and reassuring.

"I'd smash Johnny's face if he dared say one mean thing about you or your family. I wouldn't let him hurt you, Melissa."

Melissa gently released her hand from his grasp. "Well, thanks," she said. "But what about Daniel? Nobody stands up to Johnny when he ridicules Daniel."

"Hey, I've told Johnny to cool it lots of times. But what can I do? I'm not the guy's father," Chris retaliated.

"Why would you want to hang around with someone like that?" demanded Melissa.

"I don't anymore. Honest."

Touched by his sincerity, Melissa smiled at him. "Does that mean you might consider going out with me?" Chris asked in his most charming manner.

"No," Melissa said emphatically. "It means . . . I think we can be friends."

"That will do for now," Chris said with his impish grin. "But I've just begun to fight."

That night she wrote Anna, "I must be crazy. I might have spent a winter dating an absolutely gorgeous guy who's nuts about me. President of the senior class. Captain of the football team. Every girl in town would kill for his attention. And honestly, Chris really is a nice guy. So why am I pining away for the violin player?"

During January and February, Melissa was either rehearsing her stage role or practicing violin. After their scene in the cafeteria, she no longer felt a need to avoid Chris. The truth was, even if she had wanted to date him, there would have been no time. After winter break, the teachers really began to pile on the homework, and Mr. Dennis scheduled long weekend rehearsals on both Saturdays and Sundays. Then, to her surprise, Melissa was selected as one of two soloists for the school orchestra's winter concert. She was so proud to have been singled out from all the other fine musicians that Melissa approached her violin study with new zeal and increased her practice time by at least an hour a day. She also had another motive for her new-found dedication. Secretly, she wanted to outshine the other soloist—Daniel Goodman. As much as her violin playing was a source of pleasure, it also was a constant reminder of her need to compete with such an infuriating boy.

Although she and Daniel rehearsed *Romeo and Juliet* like professional actors, off-stage Daniel remained aloof and it hurt Melissa. She tried not to dwell on those feelings. Instead, she found herself thinking more and more about being Jewish. What had once been total indifference was now a mixture of pride, fear, and curiosity. She still wouldn't dare approach her parents or even talk to her grandparents on the phone about it. Her sudden interest in Judaism might arouse their suspicion, and she refused to betray Daniel—although she was no longer certain he deserved her loyalty. As the concert approached, she was feeling more competitive than ever.

The winter concert was a major school event. Along with family and friends, the entire student body was required to attend the evening concert. "It may be your only chance to perform in public this year," Mrs. O'Hara kept telling her students. "You must keep rehearsing up to the very last second."

The night of the concert, students, faculty, friends, and family flocked into the auditorium. Johnny took a seat with the rest of his football buddies at the back of the recital hall. Chris and Kathy sat with their parents in front near Melissa's mom and dad.

Melissa's solo was the third piece on the program. As she approached center stage, a hush fell over the crowd. She played a light and airy waltz. As Melissa's nimble fingers and confident bow pressed the strings of her violin, she fully understood that all those long and often tedious hours of repetition were about these few glorious moments on stage. Afterward, thunderous applause, whistles, and cheers filled the auditorium. Her face beamed with accomplishment as she peeked down at her proud mother and dad sitting in the first row.

Daniel was next. His sonata was technically more difficult, but it was slow and a lugubrious melody, not a charming crowd pleaser like Melissa's. At his conclusion, he earned a polite response. Melissa had imagined she would savor this moment, but now as Daniel took his bow, her heart reached out to him. She was pleased to see two members of the audience rise to give him a standing ovation.

At the reception, the two soloists were escorted into an adjacent room for pictures. After the local newspaper photographer made his exit, Chris rushed toward them. "Wow! You were sensational," he told Melissa. He extended his hand to Daniel. "You, too."

Daniel stood there amazed. "Thanks, Chris. It's nice of you to say so."

Suddenly, Johnny appeared. His mouth was stuffed with chocolate cake. "Boring!" he announced. "Only good part is the food."

"Come on, Johnny. Be nice. It takes years of study to play like that," Chris responded.

"Well, looks like you've wasted your time, Goodman," Johnny continued. "Nobody came to cheer but some old lady."

"That's my grandmother," Daniel coldly informed him.

"Well, she has lousy taste in boyfriends. Who was the old geezer next to her?" Johnny asked.

"You are so rude, Johnny! For your information, Gus was once a professional baseball player," said Melissa with obvious disdain. Still, she refused to let Johnny McGraw ruin this magical night. "Now he coaches Daniel," she added. "You should be so lucky."

"No thanks, let your Jew keep the old nigger for himself." Johnny started to turn, but Chris grabbed him by the arm and suddenly had him pinned to the ground.

"You can't talk to people like that," Chris said and spat in Johnny's face. "Another racist comment like that and you're gonna end up toothless."

"Hey, Chris, old buddy, lighten up. I was just making with some humor. You know me, always the wise guy," said Johnny, winking up at his pal.

Chris heaved a sigh of disgust and let go of Johnny's wrists. As Chris started to get to his feet, Johnny lunged at him, using a wrestler's hold to lift him off the ground. Chris lost his balance and fell backwards, knocking his head against the linoleum floor. He lay there stunned, unable to move, his eyes fluttering closed. Melissa screamed and knelt next to Chris. She glanced at the others for help. But Johnny pointed at Daniel and shrieked, "This is all your fault."

Daniel glared with contempt as he wildly swung his left fist at the side of Johnny's head, but, ducking the blow, Johnny seized Daniel's wrist and pushed the violin player's fingers backwards until Daniel gasped in pain. Then Daniel managed to throw his right fist into Johnny's face. At that moment, Melissa's parents rushed into the room with Chris's father. They all heard Melissa crying and Daniel scream in agony.

More than anything, Melissa wanted to be at the hospital with Chris and Daniel, but her father insisted that she wait at home.

"No one wants a nosy teenager milling around an emergency room pestering the nurses all night," he said. "We'll keep calling, honey."

Melissa stopped pleading to go to the hospital only after her dad learned that Chris had regained consciousness and appeared unhurt. "Chris's dad said the doctor ordered him to stay overnight for observation, but it looks like he'll be discharged tomorrow morning after one last examination. He should be OK," he comforted his daughter.

It wasn't until the next morning that Melissa learned any news concerning Daniel Goodman. Before going to school, she called his home.

"Mrs. Goodman, this is Melissa Jensen. How's Daniel?"

"Oy Guttenyu," Mrs. Goodman mumbled in Yiddish. "The poor child. So much pain. Last night, the doctor set his hand in a cast and afterward sent him home with me about 2 A.M. I don't know what that doctor could have been thinking. Those pain pills were worthless. My Daniel was in agony for hours. Just about twenty minutes ago, he finally dozed off to sleep." The sick woman's wheezing punctuated every phrase. "They're worried about nerve damage, but whatever it takes, I'll get him good as new," she wept.

Melissa left her house feeling so helpless. At school, she made every attempt to ignore Johnny, who was trying to give the impression to all his buddies that his own injury was just an annoying bruise. She did observe, however, that the flesh around both his eyes was discolored and badly swollen, and heavy white bandages protected his broken nose.

The first bell had not yet rung, and Johnny, surrounded by a crowd in the hallway, was describing his version of last night's events. He didn't know Melissa was at the water fountain behind him. "When my old man showed up at the hospital last night, he took one glance at me and grunted, 'The other kid better look worse!' When he heard it was two of 'em, he got off my back for making him get outta bed." Johnny paused. "Still beats me why Chris turned on me like that."

"Doesn't make sense," someone called out.

Johnny's tone became belligerent. "It's that snot from New York," he snarled. "From the first day she showed up, Chris has had a thing for her. I guess he thought he'd show off. What a bozo. It's obvious she has the hots for the lousy Jew. Who can figure taste? The kike's such a nerd!" Even a broken nose didn't prevent Johnny McGraw from making that hideous cackling sound.

Melissa shuddered. Actually, Melissa was tempted to break Johnny's nose a second time—or at the very least, put him in his place. But she sensed the group around him did not want to hear the truth. Certainly, they would never take her word over his. Besides, she wanted Johnny McGraw to face the consequences of his actions. But how could she make an example of him and at the same time, make the others more aware of their prejudice?

As she walked down the hall to her first period class, Melissa heard Mrs. Peters call to her from the principal's office. "Would you mind coming into my office for a few minutes, Melissa?"

Melissa sat across from the vice-principal and listened carefully as Mrs. Peters explained that the school board wanted a written explanation for last night's incident. "I need you to tell me everything, Melissa," Mrs. Peters said. "You were in the room when Daniel hit Johnny."

In the next thirty minutes, Melissa revealed every detail of the night before, as well as those of the preceding months. No longer willing to keep silent, she repeated all of Johnny's awful comments. She described the locker incident and the fear Daniel had instilled in her. "But slowly, I've changed," Melissa argued. "When Kathy seemed so indifferent, it infuriated me. I told her so. I also told Chris. In some ways, I blame myself for what happened last night. If I had come to you in the beginning, Chris would never have attacked Johnny because this whole problem would have been out in the open. Instead, Daniel is in horrible pain. What if he doesn't heal properly? The violin is such a demanding instrument. And he wants to go to Julliard."

Melissa burst into tears. Mrs. Peters looked very perplexed. "I'm truly sorry it took you this long to come to me," Mrs.

Peters said. "You're right. We could have avoided a lot of suffering."

"But I was scared and, at first, I thought, 'If I don't get involved, and make a big deal about it, things would be OK,'" Melissa explained.

Without another word, Mrs. Peters went to her bookcase and picked out a worn book of quotations. The cloth cover was frayed. Mrs. Peters opened it and pointed to the top of one of the pages. "This is a statement by a Protestant clergyman named Martin Niemoller," Mrs. Peters said quietly. As Melissa read silently, Mrs. Peters recited the quotation by heart.

> In Germany, the Nazis came for Communists, and I did not speak up because I was not a Communist. Then they came for the Jews, and I did not speak up because I was not a Jew. Then they came for the trade unionists, and I did not speak up because I was not a trade unionist. Then they came for the Catholics, and I was a Protestant. Then they came for me. By that time, there was no one left to speak up.

Afterward, all Mrs. Peters said was, "I think you should memorize it too," and handed Melissa the faded book.

Later that morning, Melissa cornered Rob Kingston. She wanted him to know about her meeting with Mrs. Peters. She told him she hoped Daniel wouldn't feel betrayed.

"Too much has happened," he said. "Daniel can't expect us to remain silent any longer."

In the afternoon, Mrs. Peters convened a special school assembly and addressed the issue of fighting on school grounds. She did not name names or make any accusations.

She also promised immediate expulsion to any student making racist remarks. Afterward, Melissa saw Johnny follow Mrs. Peters into her office.

By the end of the last period Johnny was waiting for his friends in the parking lot, making fun of Mrs. Peters's idea of punishment.

Melissa went home, outraged. "All Johnny got was a simple reprimand," she cried to her parents. "Chris might have been killed and Daniel may never play the violin again. How can they let that creep walk away? Where's the justice?"

"But didn't the boys attack first?" her father reminded her. "And as far as the graffiti on the locker, there is no proof that Johnny wrote it."

Melissa continued her fuming. She wasn't the only one. After her brother's accident, Kathy wanted to have nothing to do with Johnny. "I can't believe I laughed at his jokes!" she confided to Melissa. "I feel so guilty!"

"We're all to blame," Melissa answered her. "You. Me. Chris. Rob. Even Daniel."

8

Melissa Steps Up to Bat

THE EVENING AFTER THE CONCERT, Melissa's grandmother called her.

"So, darling, how was it? Your grandfather and I were thinking about you every moment. We're so proud. I'm sure you stole their hearts."

Melissa told the whole story. She even described her meeting with Mrs. Peters. Afterward, she meekly added, "Don't laugh at me, but I've made a decision. When I return to New York, I want to learn about my religion. How can I defend myself against bigotry if I don't know who I am?"

At first, Mr. Dennis wanted to postpone the play, but Daniel reassured his director. "I'm fine, sir. I can work around this silly cast."

To make Daniel's injury seem less obtrusive, Mr. Dennis

reblocked much of the staging of the play. By the day before opening, Daniel seemed so at ease playing the part in a cast that Melissa almost forgot about it. Only one brief moment, the scene before Romeo exits from Juliet's bedroom window, still bothered her.

Bidding his love, Juliet, goodbye, the hero, Romeo, must exclaim: "Farewell. Farewell. One kiss and I'll descend." Originally, Daniel had been instructed to put his arms around Melissa and kiss her gently. Now, maneuvering his body with the cast made the scene awkward. Melissa was certain they both looked clumsy on stage, but she made no comments. At this late date, she did not want Daniel to feel self-conscious. "It's only for a couple of seconds," she told herself. "Maybe I'm the one who's self-conscious."

To everyone's delight, the night of the performance Melissa and Daniel proved themselves the perfect "star-crossed lovers." By the death scene, Melissa could hear the audience weeping and imagined everyone reaching for a tissue. Afterward, the praises flowed. Even Mr. Dennis could not find enough superlatives for his leading lady. "Bravo! Sensational! Absolutely breathtaking," he exclaimed. "I'll confess it now. I was worried about that one scene where you two kiss on the balcony, but you knew exactly what to do."

Melissa smiled. "I never planned it. It just happened," she admitted. "I think I really surprised Daniel."

Rather than wait for her Romeo to embrace her, what she had done was to suddenly cup his face in her hands and kiss him. The tender gesture enthralled the audience. For Melissa, it was the only time she had not been acting the part.

Melissa's parents extended a special invitation to the actors and crew to join them for a cast party at their home on Willow Lane. Leading their blindfolded daughter into the grand ballroom, Melissa's mother and father removed the kerchief, and Melissa let out a shrill scream.

"This is awesome!" she yelled. Her mother had painted banners with scenes from *Romeo and Juliet*. The faces on the young lovers were those of Daniel and Melissa. Melissa's only disappointment was Daniel's absence. He declined the invitation because he had already made other plans with cousins who had driven from Kansas City to see the play.

At school the next morning, when Melissa described her mother's art work, Daniel looked genuinely touched. "What a tribute!" he remarked. "Good thing we didn't blow it," he said with a smile. Suddenly, he was pointing at her with his good hand. "That was pretty sneaky of you. I never even saw it coming." Melissa looked puzzled. "Don't play coy with me," he teased. "We never rehearsed the scene like that. But wow! What a moment. I almost forgot to climb out the window."

She realized he was referring to the kiss and blushed. She knew it had been a bold move. "I'm sorry. I didn't mean to break your concentration," she replied.

"Don't apologize. It was brilliant."

With that last comment, he waved to his pal, Rob and joined him down the hall.

"Since the brawl," she thought to herself, "he's been friendlier."

"But only to a point," she whined later to Jill on the phone.

Her savvy New York girlfriend dismissed the complaint. "Hey, Mel. Get with it. You're a modern woman. You don't need to wait for a male to make the first move. You like him? Ask him out for a date."

Several times, Melissa courageously picked up the telephone and dialed Daniel's number, but at the sound of the first ring, she slammed down the receiver. It's not that she was embarrassed to ask a boy out for a Saturday evening. But Daniel was different. She had such deep feelings for him. How could she risk a flat rejection?

Except for her father's comedy premiere at the college and that her mother was teaching her how to drive the car, the last ten weeks of school promised to be fairly boring for Melissa. No recital, no play, and certainly nothing in the romance department. True, since the fight, Melissa and Chris had become good friends. They sat together at lunch every noon, and now that he understood her feelings for him were strictly platonic, she even accepted his rides to and from school. But for Melissa the routine had become monotonous, and she began to mark the days until she put Henryville behind her.

"What about your birthday next week?" her mother reminded her. "I always thought March tenth was your favorite day of the year."

Melissa shrugged. In her present mood, even a birthday wasn't much of a consolation prize. After all, the day would come and she would still be stuck in Henryville. Her real "Sweet Sixteen" birthday luncheon with all her girlfriends from New York City would take place in early June. March tenth was but a mere formality.

Three days before her actual birthday, a hefty UPS package arrived from her grandparents in New York. She ripped it open and found two beautiful silver boxes tied with white satin ribbon. First she unsealed the pink envelope:

Our Dearest Melissa,
    We shall miss spending your birthday with you, but we believe we have devised the perfect present.

Since you want to learn about your Jewish roots, we thought what better way to start your education than with the story of a courageous queen. So, Melissa, in one package you'll find the story of Esther. It is also called the megillah and chanted in the synagogue every year at Purim. Read it very carefully. We think after your recent ordeal, you will discover a special connection.

Melissa opened the smaller package. As she flipped through the glossy, illustrated pages, she found the wicked Haman in his triangular hat. Melissa picked up the letter again.

But the other package is equally important. Grandpa and I had so much fun choosing it! On Purim, it is the custom for everyone to wear a costume. We visited that theatrical shop on Broadway you love so much and put together this exotic outfit. We know how much you love to "dress up" and hope you approve of our selection. Naturally, we want Mom and Dad to take you to hear the megillah and already phoned our neighbor who has family in Kansas City. She said they have quite a celebration out there. Last year, the cantor came in a gorilla suit! Wouldn't it be something if Mom and Dad wore a costume, too?

Of course, this is the real coincidence. Just by chance, Erev Purim falls out on your birthday. We couldn't have chosen a better date. Happy Birthday, darling! We'll be thinking of you.

All our love,

Grandma and Grandpa Janiwitz

"The idea is absolutely fantastic," cooed Melissa as she examined the exquisite white silk sheath, transparent veil, and gold sandals. While she ran to her bedroom to try on the outfit, her father retired to his study. Meanwhile, her mother, who savored any artistic challenge, was already mentally sketching a design for two hamantaschen costumes. Dressed in her Queen Esther attire, Melissa came downstairs to model for her parents. Then she quietly sat down in the soft leather sofa in her father's study and read her birthday present. Meanwhile, her father worked at his desk in silence.

Afterward, she remarked to her father, "You know, Dad, if I had known this story before coming to Henryville, I don't believe I could have remained silent. I would have known better."

Michael Jensen looked up in astonishment. His mother's words had come back to haunt him. "Your grandmother always warned me, but I never believed her," he told Melissa. "She said I was a fool to think changing my name would make any difference. She kept telling me that no matter how hard I pretended to be someone else, the anti-Semites would never let me forget." He paused to reflect and then added, "She was right, but it took you, Melissa, to convince me."

Purim services at the synagogue in Kansas City were festive, indeed! The costumes were outrageous, and the commotion of noisy *gragers* and squealing children added to the frenzied spirit of the evening. She didn't understand the Hebrew, but as the rabbi introduced each section of the megillah reading, Melissa smiled knowingly recalling the passages she had read earlier in the week.

Afterward, among hundreds of strangers, she saw one familiar face. "Daniel!" she called out excitedly.

"Melissa?"

She knew she had startled him. "Uh-huh," she smiled.

"Why are you here?"

"Same reason you are. To hear the megillah."

"But you're not Jewish."

"Yes, I am."

Daniel looked confused. "But your mom's Christmas party?"

"It's involved," is all Melissa told him. "Believe me. I'm Jewish." Suddenly, Daniel was laughing. "What's so funny?" she asked him indignantly.

"When we first met, and you were coaching me at my grandmother's, I had such a crush on you. I couldn't think about anyone else," Daniel said.

Melissa smiled with pleasure. "Wow! I liked you the very first time we met at the college," she said. "Why didn't you call me up for a date?"

"You were always hanging around with Chris and Johnny."

"Never Johnny!" Melissa insisted.

"And I didn't want to get serious with someone who isn't Jewish," Daniel said.

Melissa rolled her eyes. "My grandmother would approve of you," she laughed. All the while, she heard Jill's voice inside her head whispering, "This is your moment, Mel. Don't blow it. Ask him out now!"

A statuesque girl with long silky jet-black hair suddenly grabbed Daniel's free hand. "There you are!" she exclaimed. "Everyone thought you disappeared."

"Tracy, meet Melissa. She played Juliet."

"Hi!" the lovely girl replied. "I came to the show to see Danny. You were outstanding, Melissa. I mean you had me crying like a baby. Do you want to be a professional actress?"

As the three stood there chatting, it suddenly dawned on Melissa. Daniel Goodman had a girlfriend.

With the warm winds of late March came spring training on campus. After school, Melissa enjoyed sitting in the bleachers and watching Gus drill the college's baseball team. After practice, he'd graciously pitch her a few balls. To Melissa's disappointment, Daniel, whose hand would not be free of a cast until summer, did not attend these practices. Still, Melissa looked forward to her time alone with Gus. She loved when he reminisced about his years in baseball.

"Maybe the greatest one of all was a fella named LeRoy Paige. They called him Satchel. A real crowd pleaser. Just like Babe Ruth. Why they'd advertise in the papers, days in advance, just to let the fans know Satchel was on his way. And believe me, this man had a whip for a right arm." Gus paused and looked thoughtful. "Ya gotta wonder. All the records might have been different if there had been integrated teams back then."

"That must have been awful!" Melissa declared.

"Sure, it was awful," Gus admitted. "We were banned from the major leagues and made to feel like second-class citizens. But we were dedicated to the game. If we had just felt sorry for ourselves, none of us would have amounted to much of anything. That's what I've been trying to tell Daniel. Stay focused. If he had taken my advice, he wouldn't be sitting out this season."

"But Johnny goaded him," Melissa argued in Daniel's defense.

"I suppose I always knew it would come to this," Gus said. "That McGraw is bad news. Of course, most of the other kids are no better. Indifference is just another form of bigotry."

"Since the fight, I've gotten to know Chris a lot better, and I don't believe he's prejudiced," Melissa said with conviction.

"After that brawl, I wouldn't think so. But it took a long time coming and there you go. It's a lot like those old, white ball clubs. We knew they admired us. We even knew they believed the rules were lousy." Gus shrugged. "I suppose, for the white players, it was just easier to look the other way. I know it's a bad pun, but the truth is, no one was willing to go to bat for us. In the end, we all got a rotten deal."

March passed into April and April into May. The Henryville landscape came alive with the promise of an early summer. Lawns were green and lush. Trees and flowers were in full bloom. The temperature was slowly climbing, and spring fever was definitely in the air. Most high school seniors were absolutely giddy with anticipation as prom night approached. But sadly, nothing else at school changed. Although Chris seldom spoke to him, Johnny remained very popular with everyone else. Meanwhile, no one but Chris was any friendlier toward Daniel.

"It's so unfair," Melissa complained to Gus one afternoon. "His teammates idolize Johnny. How can they all be so blind?"

"Just bide your time, Melissa," Gus replied. "The opportunity may just present itself for you to change a few opinions."

Melissa doubted she could do much good during prom week. All anyone talked about was the dance—that is, everyone except Rob Kingston. "I'm dead," Rob groaned to Daniel and Melissa as they walked into the cafeteria together.

Melissa, who was in a light-hearted mood, couldn't resist commenting. "Oh, Puh-leeze. Let's all cry for poor Rob. I mean he's only class valedictorian with a full scholarship to Harvard. Give us a break! What more do you want?"

"My watch." He looked distraught.

"What happened, Rob?" Daniel asked him.

"Remember yesterday when they swiped all my clothes?" Rob reminded them.

Daniel and Melissa nodded. Both tried to hide their smiles. During swimming class, someone had raided Rob's gym locker. The prank occurred every May to the least suspecting senior. Until Rob's dad arrived with dry clothes, the class valedictorian was forced to miss classes and stay in the gym in a towel and bare feet.

"Well, I was pretty cool about it, because I figured my stuff would be returned today. That's how it goes every year," Rob said.

"Your clothes aren't back?" inquired Daniel.

"Sure, the clothes are. But my grandfather's gold watch is missing. I had tucked it inside my shoe. The thing's not waterproof. It's pretty valuable and the only thing I owned of Grandpa's."

"Sounds like someone stole it," Melissa declared.

"I'm not certain. Maybe it just dropped out of the shoe. All I know is that I'm a goner. I wasn't supposed to be wearing it in school. It's an antique. Whoa! I can just hear my mother now."

"Tough break," Daniel agreed. "What did it look like? Maybe we'll see it."

After Rob's detailed description, Melissa advised him to talk to Mrs. Peters. "If it's a theft," she told him, "the school's got to know about it."

She even told Chris the story, and after their classes he helped the three of them search the school grounds. But no one found the watch.

As prom night approached, Melissa regretted that she had allowed Chris to persuade her to volunteer for the decorating committee. Without a date, it all seemed pointless. Chris never bothered to ask Melissa to be his date for the evening. He already knew she only wanted to go with Daniel. Of course, she was extremely disappointed when she learned that Daniel had no intention of going to the prom and, as usual, would be spending his weekend in Kansas City.

"I'm just fooling myself," she brooded over the telephone to Anna one evening. "Obviously, if he changes his mind, he'll take Tracy. I totally blew it," she agonized to her girlfriend in Manhattan.

"Well, at least you'll have fun with Chris on the decorating committee," Anna said in an upbeat tone. Melissa knew her girlfriend was only trying to brighten her spirits. But it didn't help make her feel any better.

The Friday afternoon before the dance Melissa dutifully fulfilled her obligation and assisted the committee. "Hey, we're just about out of masking tape," Chris yelled from the top of the twelve-foot ladder in the school gymnasium. The committee's plans to make the gym ceiling look like a starry evening was more time consuming than any of them had anticipated. They also needed more tape than anyone had estimated.

Melissa searched the supplies. "No more here, but there are a few rolls in the auditorium. We left some backstage after *Romeo and Juliet*. I'll get 'em," she hollered up to Chris.

"Hey, wait!" Chris called after her. "I'll come, too."

They opened the doors to the empty hall. Although the curtains were pulled shut, a flicker of light shone out from the tiny crack between the two panels of blue velvet drapery. "Mr. Dennis is gonna have a fit if that light has been burning long," Melissa remarked to Chris. "Do you have any idea how expensive these stage lights are?"

She and Chris ran up the stage steps. As soon as she peeled back the curtain, she saw the group of six boys sitting on the stage. Marty Bowlen was just about to deal the next hand. "Hey! What are you doing here!" one of the boys screamed at them.

"What do you mean, us? What are you doing?" Melissa demanded.

"What's it look like?" said Johnny. "We're having a friendly game of poker. Want to join us, Chris? You used to like our company."

"You know gambling on school grounds isn't too smart," said Chris.

"Ah, next week is graduation! We're almost out of this stinkin' joint," Johnny bragged.

"Yeah," piped up Marty Bowlen. "What are they gonna do to us?" The gang of six all laughed.

"Well, you guys can mess around, but I'm looking forward to walking down the aisle in my cap and gown." Chris remained calm.

"I'm disappointed, Chris. When I smashed you down on the ground," taunted Johnny, "I must have jiggled some of those brain cells. If I didn't know better, I'd say you've turned yella."

Chris turned in disgust, but Melissa was still watching as Johnny held his hands up to his armpits and waved his elbows while clucking like a chicken. That's when she saw the wrist-watch on Johnny's arm.

"Nice watch," she commented. "Where did you get it?"

"Won it in a poker game. What's it to you, anyway?" he snarled at her.

"Nothing," Melissa replied. "Just that I like old watches. Can I see it for a minute?"

"This is pricey stuff. The jeweler said 18K. Way out of your league," Johnny scoffed as he flashed the watch in Melissa's face. From Rob's description, she instantly knew it was the lost heirloom.

"You say you won it from someone in a poker game? Anyone I know?" She acted very innocent.

"Don't insult me," Johnny said. "I won it in a big time game with some professional gamblers my dad knows. We cleaned them out last December."

"Gosh, you've had it this long and I never noticed," Melissa commented.

"I thought you said you just won it the other night," Marty corrected Johnny.

Johnny bristled. "Ya got a big mouth, Bowlen. Now, shut up and deal."

"Can I join you guys?" Melissa asked sweetly. Chris gasped.

"Do yourself a favor, Melissa, and forget you ever saw us," said Marty. "Otherwise, Johnny here will rob you blind. I'm already down thirty bucks."

"Too bad your Jewish buddy, Daniel, ain't here," Johnny sneered. "Those people are all filthy rich. I wouldn't mind cleanin' him or any of those lousy Jews out of their stinkin' money."

"You're in for it now," Chris threatened him. "Come on, Melissa, let's get out of here."

He pulled at her arm, but Melissa did not budge. She glared straight at Johnny. "Well, it's your lucky day, Johnny. It just so happens I'm Jewish. You think you can clean me out?" Her eyes never left his.

"Figures," he mumbled under his breath while glaring back at her.

"Hey, Johnny, I think you've just been challenged," Marty said in utter amazement.

"Unless McGraw's too scared," Melissa goaded.

Johnny slowly opened his lips into a sinister smile. "It will be my pleasure." he said.

Before she could take a seat, Chris pulled her aside. "Are you crazy? I told you before. Nobody beats Johnny. Why are you doing this?" Chris looked frantic.

"Somebody's got to," is all she said. "Do you have any money?"

He opened his wallet and looked at his sixty dollars. "This is my prom money," he said nervously.

"Don't worry," Melissa told him. "I'll give it back to you."

"But what if you get caught?" Chris asked.

"I've got to take this chance, Chris. That's Rob Kingston's watch. This is my one chance to show those guys what a creep Johnny really is." Melissa looked determined.

"So, go tell Mrs. Peters!" Chris exclaimed.

"If I lose—"

"Lose?" Chris gulped. "I thought you said my money's safe."

"I think I can beat him," Melissa said reassuringly. "Now get back to the gym. If anyone asks, tell them I had to leave for a while."

"You could get into a lot of trouble," Chris said gravely.

"I know."

With its billowy clouds and glittering silver stars, the gymnasium looked like a small corner of heaven. Almost an hour later, Melissa appeared at the gym door. Chris was standing on top of a ladder hanging a crescent moon. She called up to him and held her hand high in the air, waving three twenty dollar bills. Chris rushed down the ladder.

"You beat him?" he whispered to her.

"Every penny," Melissa told him.

"How much?"

Melissa shrugged. "After it was over, I took your sixty and left the rest on the table. I don't want any of his grubby money. But Rob Kingston owes me big time." She giggled and dangled the watch in front of him.

"Wow! I'm impressed," Chris said. "What about the others?"

"They're plenty sore at Johnny. They were all in on the prank, but none of them ever saw the watch except Johnny. Marty actually called him a thief to his face! At first, I thought Johnny was gonna try to rip Marty's heart out, but all of 'em ganged up on Johnny. I loved watching him try to worm his way out of it. Finally, he just ran out like the gutless coward he is. Trust me. When the word gets out, Johnny McGraw is history. Still, the whole thing doesn't make much sense." Melissa looked puzzled.

"What do you mean?" asked Chris. "We got our revenge."

"Sure," she said. "But how come those guys think a thief is any worse than a racist? Why did they idolize the creep for so long?"

"Hey, listen. I'm as much to blame as the rest of 'em. I always figured Johnny's jokes were harmless. Now, I know better." The deep shame in Chris's blue eyes made Melissa sad. Yet, at that moment, she only wanted to savor the sweetness of her victory.

"Hey, we have to find a telephone," she shouted.

Melissa called Rob from the school pay phone. Ten minutes later, he was running into the gymnasium. Melissa and Chris huddled with him in a quiet corner and told him all that had happened. After he strapped the watch back on his wrist, he hugged them both with gratitude.

"Hey, Buddy," Chris laughed as he backed away from Rob's big bear hug. "I didn't do anything. Thank Melissa."

Rob looked at Melissa. "I've got to catch Daniel on the phone before sunset. Just wait until he hears this. I keep telling him he's missing out on a good thing. You're really remarkable." Melissa became flustered and made no reply. "See you both at the prom?" Rob asked casually as he approached the door.

While Chris nodded, Melissa mumbled under her breath, "I'm not going." She didn't think Rob had heard her, but he had.

Melissa planned for an uneventful Saturday night. Although her parents had offered to take her out to dinner and a movie, she chose to stay home and mope with a mushroom pizza in front of the TV. The thought of herself out with her folks on prom night was more than even she could handle. At the last moment, her parents felt so badly for their daughter that they canceled their own movie plans. It was almost ten o'clock when the telephone rang in the den. Her parents were waiting for the local news, and Melissa was closest to the phone. "Daniel?" she asked, "Aren't you in Kansas City?"

"I was," he answered. "But Grandma and I rushed home after sundown. I know it's awfully sudden, and I'll understand if you refuse, but Rob convinced me I shouldn't miss the prom. I just assumed you were dating Chris. We could still catch the last couple hours of the dance. What do you say?"

Melissa detected an eagerness in his voice. "But Daniel," she said. "I don't have a prom dress."

"Me, neither. I mean, I don't have a tuxedo. I figure a suit and tie will do. That is, if you don't mind."

"Well, sure. OK. I'll get ready."

Melissa slammed down the receiver, looked at her parents and screamed in ecstasy. Then she panicked. "Oh, no! Mother! What am I going to wear?"

Mother and daughter ran upstairs together to search through Anita's closet. Thirty minutes later, Melissa couldn't have appeared more radiant as Daniel escorted her down the porch steps to his car. In her mother's gold sequined cocktail dress, Melissa felt like Cinderella on her way to the ball. Still, one thought kept nagging her. As Daniel opened the car door for her, Melissa suddenly stepped aside. "Before I get in, I've got to know. Why didn't you ask Tracy?" The words just tumbled out of her mouth.

"Tracy? My cousin, Tracy Katz?" Daniel looked puzzled, and then an impish smile spread across his face. "Melissa, did you think Tracy was my girlfriend?"

Melissa silently blessed the darkness. Otherwise, she was sure Daniel would have seen her face turn several shades of red. "Forget it," she urged him and hurried into the car.

Neither Melissa nor Daniel could have predicted the greeting they received when they stepped into the gymnasium. Marty Bowlen spotted them from across the room and rushed up to them. "I've got to shake your hand, Goodman. Without a doubt, you're the luckiest guy here. I mean this girl has heart. She really put Johnny in his place. Melissa, the guys and I owe you. If he ever gives either of you any lip about being Jewish, you let me know." He winked at Melissa and turned.

Daniel and Melissa shared a special smile. Then the music changed. It was a slow dance. Even with a cast, Daniel managed to guide Melissa gracefully around the dance floor. Neither spoke, but Melissa was thinking, "He's a pretty good dancer, too."

CPSIA information can be obtained
at www.ICGtesting.com
Printed in the USA
LVHW030908030121
675537LV00009B/2088